364
a year

Sarah Riad

COPYRIGHT

ISBN 9781724030887
First edition
Cover art by Qamber Designs Media
Editing by EditElle
Proofreading by Megan Luker
Typesetting by Mermaid Publishing House

DEDICATION

To Megan
This book is for you.
One day, I'll return the favour, I promise.

THERE ARE NO SECRETS THAT TIME DOES NOT REVEAL.

—Jean Racine

Chapter ONE

I t always starts in the same way.

On the 29th of March, at 12am, I wake suddenly, gasping for air. No matter if it's the 12th time or the 89th time, I am consistently met with a wave of sickness as the dread settles into the pit of my stomach.

As I gather myself, I glance around, taking in my surroundings, doing my best to piece together the broken puzzle I'm left with. But that is where the similarities end.

The next bit is never the same.

At first, I try to figure out what has happened and where I am in the world. I have woken in the most natural of places and also in some of the strangest but I usually don't have much time to figure everything out right away, especially if there's a crowd because I have been in a car accident or supposed to have died in the blazing fire of a burning building. I've come to learn how important it is to lose the crowd, dodging any questions I don't know the answer to but what's more difficult is when people have seen my new body die. How do you explain yourself out of that one?

You don't. *You just run.*

Sometimes I wake up in a house but, as the times have changed, it's become somewhat of a rarity for it to be a pleasant wake-up. Even when it is, there's no guarantee that it will be a good life.

Once I've hidden myself from prying eyes, I look at my new body, usually beginning with my hands. You can learn so much about a person from their hands. First, do they belong to a male or female? I can usually figure it out by simply looking for the basics, such as nail varnish, jewellery, hair and the shape of the fingers. Once I've figured out the gender, I study the skin and nails. Is the skin soft and clean or are the hands tough and covered in dirt? And the nails, are they long and manicured or dirty and chipped? At this point, I can guess how I might be living this new life.

Not all things are a complete mystery to me when I first wake. I always know of two things: One is that it is always the day of my 17th birthday and another is that I will die, once again, on the day before my 18th birthday.

I know nothing else about the body I'm in. Not their name or where they're from. Sometimes, I can figure out how they died, especially if it's obvious—like a suicide or car accident—but then there are other times where I find myself surrounded by no obvious cause.

In the beginning, I would do all I could to find out who the body belonged to. I'd get to know their families and friends and sometimes I would find myself getting caught up, living as though the life belonged to me and wouldn't eventually end, as it always did. Things are different now, I no longer have the energy to care.

Now, I just wait.

I exist as quietly as possible until the day comes when it all ends again.

I can imagine you're wondering why this happens to me and I wish I had an answer. I used to spend each lifetime trying to figure out what was wrong with me. I've researched thousands of books and been quizzed by doctors with a hundred questions, but neither them or I got any of

2

answers that we needed. I've grown close to someone and confessed my secret, only to be shunned away as though I was crazy.

Since the year 1909, I have lived in 108 bodies and I have died 108 times.

This will be my 109th.

Chapter TWO

As I woke and opened my eyes, I was met with a burning sensation as warm water seeped past my eyelids. The sound of my heart beating ferociously surrounded me as my lungs felt as though they were moments from setting alight. The water rushed up my nose and down my throat as I began to see black spots in front of me. Through the blurry, almost red water, I concentrated on a bright light above me and wondered what might happen if I continued to remain under the water, but the wonder came to a desperate end as I threw my hands out of the water, trying to grasp onto anything. Finding the sides of a bathtub, I pulled myself up, desperately gasping for air.

"Are you okay? What's all that noise?" I heard a woman's voice shout followed by loud bangs against the door.

"Yes, fine," I said, noticing my English accent, "I swallowed some water by accident and choked." I spluttered, thankful to be able to breathe again.

No matter how many times you die, you never get used to it.

"Well don't be so stupid next time, Effy!" The woman spoke again, sounding irritated.

"Erm... Okay, I won't..." I said past the burn in my throat, slightly amused at the tone of her voice.

"Well I'm going to bed now, so make sure you do the same. You have school tomorrow."

"Sure..."

This was always the difficult bit; settling into the body without causing the people around me to become suspicious. I needed to act as normal as possible, as though I wasn't a complete stranger trapped in a dead girl's body.

Effy.

That was my new name, or perhaps a nickname, either way, it was a start.

I looked around me, wondering where the pink water had come from when I spotted a knife sitting in a large pool of blood on the floor beside the bath. I quickly looked down at my arms to find all the wounds had long gone.

Suicide.

I climbed out of the bath onto the chessboard-like flooring and as I grabbed a towel from a metal railing, I caught my reflection in a mirror. I pushed the dark, long hair away from my face, leaving it to fall beside me in a wet tangled mess. My skin was a pastel white, which only helped to make my blushed lips stand out, matching the colour in my cheeks. I looked deep into my new eyes, noticing how the colour reminded me of aged wood, specks of a rich brown paired with strokes of gold. I was a pretty girl, the kind of classic beauty that didn't need much makeup to help accentuate. I could already tell that appearance was important to the original Effy from the number of face creams and body fragrances that were neatly lined up on the clean bathroom shelves.

"Okay, Effy, let's go figure out who we are," I whispered to my new reflection before anxiously opening the closed door and finding a bedroom. I sighed with relief that it was empty and hurried over to the bedroom door to lock it.

The room was spacious with a weird pointed ceiling, but beneath it were thick wooden beams, wrapped in fairy lights, stretching across the length of the room and surrounded by off-white walls. In the corner of the room sat a double bed, covered in an excessive amount of grey and white pillows and a grey blanket that looked softer than clouds. In another corner hung a chair hammock, also covered in pillows. It was tidy, everything was put away and had its place. Her clothes were hung neatly in the wardrobe and books were lined up in colour order on the shelves. The dressing table in front of the bed was perfectly organised with each drawer filled with different types of makeup and decorated with more fairy lights.

I quickly began to snoop through the drawers, messing up all Effy's tidy work, finding a passport and what looked like a diary. I liked bodies like Effy and their organised ways. It made it easier for me to figure things out instead of guessing the entire time.

I opened the passport, finding an old picture of Effy staring back at me. She looked young, probably in her early teens, with chubbier cheeks and dark unruly brows.

"Ophelia Lori Garcia, born 29th of March 2001"

Throwing the passport on the bed, I pulled open the diary and looked for the most recent entry.

25 March 2018

Today was so amazing. I asked Ayden if he was coming to my birthday party this weekend and he said maybe. I know he will though, everyone is coming and he won't want to be the only person that doesn't. I am going to look so amazing in my dress. I really hope so anyway. I just wish for once he would see me in the way that he sees Brogan, Jess and

Naomi. Sometimes, I feel so ugly compared to them. Jess is so tall and slim, Naomi has the most amazing eyes and Brogan is easily the prettiest girl in school. I just hope he comes on Saturday.

Effy x

I grimaced at the words in front of me, feeling a touch of sympathy for her and silently hoping she hadn't ended her life for a boy. I continued to flip through the diary, noticing Ayden's name appear over and over again before jumping from the sound of a phone buzzing from a cabinet behind me. I grabbed it and pushed my finger to unlock it finding several notifications of people posting on my wall. It was Effy's birthday, at least it would have been. Instead, it was mine and I was 17 years old for the 109th time.

I sighed out loud as I ignored the notifications and switched the phone onto silent, noticing the time. It was already almost 1am. It wasn't unusual for me at this point to have fled and been out on the street, wondering how the life would play out, but this time, I was hesitant. My last life-time had been so rough that I wasn't sure I had it in me to run again, at least not so soon after waking. Things seemed *nice* in the new life as Effy, though I knew better than to trust first impressions.

But one night *surely* wouldn't hurt.

I turned my attention back to Effy's diary, curious to find out if it was this Ayden kid that had caused the bloody mess I would have to clean up eventually, or if someone else had played a part. From my experience, it was never just one thing that pushed a person, but a million and one things, or in my case, 108 lives.

As I flicked through the diary, I was almost disappointed that I didn't find a suicide note or even a mention of planning to do it. Whilst I knew not everyone wrote a letter or note, I really did think Effy might have.

Tired from the reading, I hid the diary under the mattress and faced the bathroom, screwing up my face at the sight of the blood highlighted by the whiteness of the bathroom. Quietly, I began to round up all the towels and bed sheets I could find to help me pretend as though none of the last few hours had happened.

This was new for me. It had been several lifetimes since I had cared enough to clean up the mess left behind by the body I had come to temporarily own.

Why haven't we left yet? Isn't it time we leave?

I ignored the questions my tired mind asked as I finished the last area of the floor. Satisfied with the job I had done, I bagged up the evidence and hid it in a packed storage cupboard in the bathroom before finding my way to a bed made of clouds.

"We'll just take a little nap," I promised myself as my eyes grew heavier and the clouds sucked me in.

I woke several hours later to a knocking at the door and the name 'Effy' being called out.

"Why is the door locked?" the voice called again and I recognised it as the same woman from the night before.

"Just getting dressed," my croaky voice called back.

"Well, hurry up. You'll be late to school and I don't need you embarrassing us again," the woman shouted before walking off in what sounded like clogs.

I rubbed my eyes and sighed loudly as I climbed out of the bed. I knew I needed to hurry and find a way out of the house, otherwise I would be forced to go back to school and I certainly didn't want to go through *that* again. I pulled open Effy's wardrobe to find every pastel colour ever created. Sky blues, perky pinks with sunny yellows, all in colour order as though a rainbow had thrown up all over it.

"There is no chance I'm going to be seen in any of this," I said out loud as I closed the door to Barbie's wardrobe and began to search through the chest of drawers, only to find more of the same. Relief washed over me as I opened the bottom drawer.

Hidden away was a drawer filled with clothes on the other end of the colour scale. I grabbed a pair of khaki jeans with a few slits in the leg and pulled on a loose black woolly jumper.

"This is more like it," I said at Effy's reflection in a floor-length mirror before the light from her phone caught my eyes.

Dad: 5 Minutes and I am coming up there and dragging you to school. Love Dad x

I pushed my feet into a pair of black ankle boots and stood by the bedroom door before grabbing a black leather jacket and searching through a handbag left beside it.

I wasn't looking for anything other than cash. I had learnt cards were trouble and would eventually get you caught on the run. Jewellery would also do the same as most jewellers wouldn't buy an item from you without taking your address anymore. Cash was the only thing you could rely on, but it was becoming more and more difficult to come across as people preferred their contactless cards and fingerprints.

As I stuffed the loose change into my back pocket, I

shoved Effy's phone into another pocket and faced the mirror one last time. "Ok, let's go meet your parents."

I could feel the usual flutter of nerves in the bottom of my stomach as I opened the bedroom door and found a long corridor with warm cream walls covered in a variety of different shaped pictures. Almost all featured my new face at some point in her last 17 years. There were also two other faces that appeared in most of the photos. One was a woman with glossy grey eyes and a smile that left you questioning its authenticity if you looked for too long. Her skin was as pale as my own, almost matching her obvious veneers, and her blonde hair sat above her shoulders in wavy curls. The other person was a man, not quite as youthful looking but, if you looked past the receding hairline and the map of wrinkles surrounding his eyes, you found a warm smile. The kind of smile that was contagious. I couldn't explain it, but he looked familiar even though I knew I had never seen him before.

Having seen the photos and parts of the house, I was curious about what was really happening in the Garcia household. On the surface, it seemed all so lovely, but nobody commits suicide because their life is lovely.

I continued to walk down the corridor, tempted to open each door I passed, but staying focused on the stairs ahead of me. I took a deep breath as I reached the first step, trying to shake off the stupid nerves.

"Effy, what is taking you so long? It's almost 9am." I jumped and knocked a picture off the wall, watching it tumble down each step until it reached the person the voice belonged to. It was the man from the pictures not looking as happy as he did in the photos, but there was still a kindness in his eyes.

"Are you feeling okay?" he said as I reached the bottom

step and picked up the smashed photo frame of Effy in her school uniform.

"Fine." I flashed a strained grin.

"Are you sure? It's just... you don't look yourself." I watched as he looked at the clothes I was wearing, probably never having seen Effy in the colour black. I knew it was risky to go against what would normally be done, but once on the streets, I needed to stay out of the way and I couldn't do that if I was dressed as a pack of highlighters.

"Yes, fine. I better go... to school." I said walking towards the door, about to pull it open.

"And there's a secret entrance from the laundry room?" He looked over to me with his eyebrows nearly touching.

"No..." I spluttered as his eyes watched me curiously. It was obvious I was out of practice. "I just needed to grab something, but don't worry, I'll be quick."

"Right..." He watched me as I grabbed the first thing within sight, which happened to be a pair of white socks.

"You needed my socks... okay then. Shall we get going then?"

"Oh, so you're coming with me?" I asked, silently thinking of a plan B as I awkwardly held onto the socks.

"Effy, are you sure you're okay? We've been driving to school together every day since you were 11 years old."

Come on Effy, we are better than this.

"Of course, I was just joking...Dad."

He nodded, still as curious but seemingly satisfied with my answer.

"Don't forget your bag." He pointed to a black handbag by the front door before walking out.

Ok, plan B is that we let him drop us to the school and once he is gone, we just leave.

"Effy?" Mr. Garcia called out again.

"Coming!" I shouted as I swung the bag over my shoulder and hurried down the corridor and out of the house.

"Happy Birthday, Effy!" I was greeted by Mr. Garcia, proudly showing off a white convertible parked on the drive with a huge pink bow covering the front window.

"Wow," I said trying to recall another life where I'd been given a car, but this was the first time.

A first.

Now that was a rare word in my lives.

One of the things you come to learn after looking at life through a lot of different eyes is just how lucky very few people were. Effy woke up in a beautiful home with the knowledge that people cared about her and wanted her to have the nicer things and though there was far more to life than just nice things, it was not as common as people like to think.

"You don't like it?" Mr. Garcia spoke quietly as the happiness drained from his face leaving only disappointment.

"No, of course I do. Thank you so much... Dad." I said awkwardly but trying as hard as I could to seem the right amount of grateful. I may have lived for over a hundred years, but it didn't mean I had great people skills. The ones I did have had long gone rusty.

There was something about Mr. Garcia, though. I felt like I wanted to care about him. I just couldn't for the life of me figure out why.

Whether it be sympathy or I had genuinely gone mad, I found myself giving him a hug, the first one I had given in about 17 years.

"Look, I'm sorry about your mother rushing off this morning. You know she's just distracted at the moment with work. She doesn't say it enough, but she does love you very much, she's just not the best at showing it." I smiled up at him as he moved his arm to my shoulder, gently squeezing every few seconds.

"I know…" I lied, "and honestly, thank you so much for the car. It's a really great gift."

Shame you can't keep it.

Mr. Garcia smiled before kissing my forehead and for a second, I almost let myself enjoy the moment.

Snap out of it. You are not Effy.

"Ok, so do I get to drive this fancy new car or is it just something to keep that very pink bow on?" I pointed out, eager to drive such a car.

"Of course and you love pink!" he replied, offering me the keys with a smile, but I could see he was sad that the moment had ended.

"Yes, so I've noticed…" I whispered. "Before we head off, would you mind putting the postcode into the SatNav? I'd hate to break it on the first day of having it."

"Good idea," he said as he climbed into the car and began pressing the buttons. I left him to it, thankful he didn't ask why I didn't know the route after six years and instead begun to rummage through the bag I had picked.

School pass, driver's licence, lipsticks, perfume… blurgh, stinky perfume, more lipsticks, ahh… these look cool.

I pulled out a pair of tortoise-shell sunglasses looking slightly worn with a few scratches on the black lenses.

"Well, I never thought I would see you wearing those. I'm surprised you even keep them on you." Mr. Garcia said with a soft smile as he climbed out of the car and began to pull off the hideous bow.

"Why?" I said putting the glasses on and admiring the bronzed glow it gave everything, "These are really nice."

"In that case, you must be ill as you didn't say that when I gave them to you. You told me off for giving you a pair of my old, crappy sunglasses."

I shrugged my shoulders, "fashion changes, and every now and again, so do people."

"I think 17 is going to suit you, Effy." He smiled before opening the car door and climbing in once again.

"It should be a nice day today, but still quite chilly, so I can show you how to put the roof down if you want?"

"I just got a convertible for my birthday, it could be pouring down with rain and I'd still keep it open. How will people know it's a convertible if the roof is up?" I smiled from the driver's seat.

Mr. Garcia laughed and pulled the door shut, "Very true. Well, we better get going otherwise the kids won't see you pull up in your new car."

"Right..." I replied, remembering how much attention the car would bring, especially since I was planning on leaving as soon as Mr. Garcia had left.

I drove off and he and I continued talking. It was the most natural conversation I'd had in years. I wasn't even pretending to be Effy as we spoke, so either Effy and I had more in common than I had thought, or Mr. Garcia didn't know his daughter that well at all.

"You have now arrived at your destination," the automated female voice pointed out as I pulled into a parking space in front of a large and grand building. It didn't look like many of the schools I'd been to previously. It was tall with pointed ceilings and arched windows, similar to those you might see on a church. Around the orange bricks were cream and gold trimmings and three tall arched entrances sat beside each other. A large mix of people stood outside talking to one another as they headed to the entrances.

From kids still in uniforms with their parents dropping them off to the other sixth-formers with the privilege of wearing their own clothes.

It wasn't long before all eyes were on the white convertible and the girl just staring out of it.

"Well, here I am," I said looking over at Mr. Garcia who was pulling together his own bag.

"Indeed, we had better get going before we both get into trouble. Mr. Swieton isn't just your headmaster, he's my boss too!"

I could have laughed out loud in disbelief.

"Because you're a teacher at the same school as me... funny." I said, looking at the school building I now had to attend.

It had been a few years since I'd last been to school and whilst it hadn't been my favourite thing to do, it was a highlight compared to other things I could have been doing. In the past, I had tried to take it seriously, brushing up on skills I had learnt over the years. I was fluent in French, Spanish and Latin, and could read Shakespeare without a headache. I could even play a couple of instruments, though I was probably a bit rusty now. It seemed silly to study the same thing over and over again when there was very little point, but sometimes it was an easy distraction.

We climbed out of the car and I followed Mr. Garcia through the crowds of kids as we approached the entrance, recognising the confusion on the faces of those that obviously had known Effy.

"I best get inside. Have a great day and I will see you here after school," he said, kissing me on the forehead and walking off inside.

I sighed and looked up at the stairs leading to a day of absolute misery before walking past a group of sixth formers, who were obviously the 'cool kids'. As I passed by, I could hear their whispers.

"Is that Effy Garcia?"

"Who does she think she is?"

"Daddy can get her the car, but obviously not any style."

"I mean, who's funeral?"

"Typical Effy, trying too hard to stand out, as usual."

I quietly laughed to myself as I approached the entrance to City Hill School & Sixth Form.

Welcome back to school, Effy.

Chapter THREE

The first time I ever went to school was in 1984. My name was Taylor Reed and I was a Junior in Westview High School in Pittsburgh, Pennsylvania. Though I had read about schools and seen them from afar, I didn't really know what to expect. In fact, I was not often expected to attend school since, in many places around the world, school was not compulsory after you were 16 years old. Even when a lifetime did come along where school was a possibility, I somehow always managed to get out of it but this time, I decided to give it a try.

With over seventy years experience of being a 17-year-old and having lived in thirty-five countries, I was pretty confident that I had nailed being a teenager. I'd experienced the good and the bad and survived, but none of that could prepare me for school.

I woke up as Taylor feeling pinned down, pressed into something sharp. As my vision cleared, I began to notice the pieces of glass stuck in the seat in front of me. A burning smell of rubber lingered in the air just like the grey smoke that surrounded me. As I registered what had happened, I spotted a woman in the driver's seat looking a lot less impacted with just a bloody nose (and what doctors would describe as shock). Knowing I wouldn't have long before she remembered me in the background and we would be joined by the concerned passers-by, I looked down in the darkness at the parts of metal wedged inside me. There was no pain, there never was, but if I didn't remove it myself, I would cause hysteria when the medics watched an actual miracle take place as my wound healed without leaving so much of a scratch. I only ever healed when I woke up from whatever death had just taken place. For the rest of my 364 days, I would hurt and bleed just as I was supposed to, though I could never die. Not before the 28th of March, anyway.

I pulled myself away from the metal and watched the skin of my stomach quickly mend itself. Pulling my top down, I noticed the stains of blood and rips in my clothes, not to mention the pool of blood on the seat beside me. I sighed quietly and looked around my feet for something sharp. Settling for a loose piece of broken glass from the window, I raised my T-shirt once more before holding my breath and screwing up my face as the glass sliced into my skin. There was no way anyone was going to believe I survived a car accident if I was covered in blood without a scratch on me. I had to make it believable to avoid any doubt.

"Taylor!" the woman in front of me shouted, soon followed with a scream, "Oh my God, are you okay, baby?"

"Yes, I'm fine," I said dropping the broken glass from my hand and pulling my T-shirt down.

"Are you hurt?" she said, beginning to cry as she tried to pull at the doors.

"A little," I replied as the wound throbbed with a stinging sensation.

The woman forced her own door open before climbing out of the car and rushing over to me. Except for a bloody nose, you wouldn't have thought she had just been in a car accident as her blonde perm remained as bouncy as her blue puffed shoulders. She covered her mouth, hiding a muffled shriek as she saw me.

After a few minutes, the paramedics and fire brigade arrived, insisting that I couldn't just climb out onto the front seat to get out of the car and instead made me wait as they cut off the door beside me. Holding a blanket to my wounded side given to me by the paramedics, I was finally carried out of the car and onto a stretcher as the paramedics looked over me with surprised eyes as they expected a wound far more gruesome and life-threatening than the one I had. Despite my insisting that I was fine, I was taken to hospital in the ambulance to be given fifteen stitches before the doctors waved me off, astonished by my 'luck'.

"Not many people can say they survived a car accident as damaging as that one, Taylor. The other car had completely gone through your side of the seat," they reminded me.

We were finally released the next morning and the woman from the car, who had been confirmed as "my" mother at the hospital, arranged a taxi for us to get home.

I was under strict instructions by my new mum to spend the rest of the day resting in my new bedroom, which suited me fine as it gave me time to find information on Taylor.

It might come as a bit of surprise at how much can be found out about a person from just their simple possessions. Nowadays, the messages on a person's phone will have conversations, varying from the generic "can you get some milk?" to the secret "I think I'm in love with my sister's boyfriend". On social media and chat messengers, you find the pictures to match the faces. In the notes section, you find passwords and reminders. Calendars reveal birthdays and emails help too, depending on the person. Not many teenagers use an email these days unless it's for a discount code.

Then, when you piece it all together, you sometimes know the person just as a friend might.

However, it has only been that easy for the last few years. In 1984, mobile phones weren't all that common, and even if you had one, there was no way you'd find it useful aside from making a phone call. Back in those days, I had to rely on diaries, which in turn are now very uncommon.

Taylor's diary wasn't the most helpful, but she also wasn't the most difficult person to figure out. She had a good life, nice enough parents, a beautiful home and all the clothes and makeup an 80's teen could ever need. Her diary told me all the same, her dad worked hard in New York whilst her mum stayed at home taking care of her. She liked someone named Jake who was a senior, and she was fairly confident she was going to be crowned Prom Queen at her Junior Prom this year. Being Taylor Reed was going to be easy—or so I thought.

Soon came the day where I was finally allowed to leave the house and return to school. I started the day getting ready, picking out the perfect outfit that I knew Taylor would wear and fixed my bouncy curls perfectly.

Something that should be known about me is that there are times when I do enjoy a life, albeit it has been a while, but every now and again, I find myself forgetting the countdown and it has always been because I'm doing something I've never done before.

So off I went to school, full of confidence and an eagerness to make the most of what I thought was going to be a great life. Except it really wasn't a great life and I was not nearly close to mastering the know-how to being a 17 year old.

In the space of four months, I had completely and utterly ruined poor Taylor's life. No longer were we popular—or even liked for that matter—and you can definitely assume I didn't make Prom Queen.

How? How was it possible that everything could have gone so wrong when it was supposed to be so easy? Taylor was the perfect pre-made life. All I had to do was say and do the right things and it would have been fine.

Well, I tried, I kept trying even when I knew I was failing miserably. My first mistake was thinking other teens would be stupid enough to not see the differences between old Taylor and the new one. I played the cute card, the bitch card, the I'll-do-anything-please-just-accept-me card, but quickly, Taylor's friends knew something was wrong. I'd become desperate and was trying far too hard. Soon enough, none of Taylor's friend wanted anything to do with me and I became the kid that sat in the classroom at lunch because she had nowhere else to go, the kid that people would walk past and whisper about. In four months, I went from Prom Queen to nobody.

Never had I felt so humiliated. When the day of my death arrived, it was greeted with absolute relief and with each lifetime that followed Taylor Reed, I prayed that having to attend a school would never be an option and if I had to, then I would wish for the body of a kid who was already a loner and not anyone that was considered 'popular'. You can't fall down the social ladder if you are already at the bottom.

Back in the life of Effy and I was the first to my history lesson, finding the perfect desk in the far right corner, next to a window overlooking the school car park. I looked through my new handbag trying to find a notepad and pen, but instead only being able to find a beauty magazine, more makeup and two more bottles of equally stinky perfume.

"Excuse me?" I called to the smartly dressed teacher writing on what looked like a giant iPad screen, "Please, can I borrow a notebook and pen as I seem to have forgotten mine at home." The teacher turned to me, revealing a youthful face that I didn't expect. He looked to be more in his thirties than the fifties I had presumed.

"You want a notebook?" he scoffed with an amused facial expression.

"Yes, how else can I take notes?"

He turned his back to me again, this time reaching into a cupboard beside his desk, "Funny, as I've been asking you that question all year," he replied walking to my desk and hovering over me with a blank notebook and some pens in his hand.

"If I see one note passed around this lesson, you'll spend the rest of the week in detention. Do I make myself clear, Miss Garcia?"

I pursed my lips together, trying to hide a smile. Over a hundred lifetimes and I still wanted to do the exact opposite of what I was told.

"Crystal."

"Good," he replied, seeming smug before returning back to his screen as the other kids gathered in the room. I turned my attention to my phone, quickly going over the pictures of Effy's friends.

"Effy, what's up with you today?" I looked up at the girl approaching my desk, wondering how she wasn't yet the face of a famous beauty brand with her beautiful dark skin and bright green eyes. I wondered which one of the infamous trio she was as the other two followed behind her. These were the so-called 'friends' of Effy Garcia, but were obviously quite the opposite according to her diary.

"Nothing." I flashed a false grin before looking back down at my phone.

"Well, obviously something is up. You're dressed for a funeral!" one of the others said and as she finished she looked around waiting for laughs which she didn't get.

"Okay, thanks for your feedback, I'll be sure to take it on board for future reference. Now, if you don't mind," I said, packing away my phone and turning to my new notebook, refusing to look at their faces.

"Oh, come, girls. She's obviously just trying to attention seek..." The red-haired and arguably prettiest of the three spoke and I knew straight away she was the ringleader of the little group. I'd had the displeasure of coming across people like her and her little minions numerous times over the years and it wasn't always in school. I hated their self-righteous attitudes and the egos that matched and I had watched them only get worse. In each decade that passed by, the mean girls got meaner, the bullies got more vindictive and the tactics used were far more damaging. These kinds of kids broke people like Effy, by pretending to be her friend all the while picking at her faults, one by one until they became open, raw wounds that she began to attack herself.

"Guess what, Effy? No one cares. Let's go, girls." The redhead finished and I was sure she was the Brogan that had appeared as much as Ayden in Effy's diary.

"And yet, you've pretty much spent the last fifteen minutes going on about what I'm wearing. I mean, stop the press — girl arrives at school wearing the colour black. Scandalous!" I finished with the mother of all smirks.

"You're actually so weird," she mocked, but I could see a curious look in her eyes.

"Girls!" The teacher interrupted the deathly stare being given to me by the trio, "Do we all get an invitation to this little meeting you're holding or perhaps you could reschedule it and get your backsides to your desks?" He finished, causing a rush of red to fill the girl's cheeks as we all noticed the classroom was now full with eyes staring over at us. There was one set I recognised instantly, even though I had never seen them before. This was the incredible Ayden West, or so Effy thought. I could see why she liked him. He had the kind of face that you felt compelled to look at, not because of his obvious good looks but because there was something about him that you couldn't quite place. His choppy dark hair was pushed to one side and as he spoke with those around him, I watched his full lips move, leading to a strong and defined grin. For a brief moment, he looked over at me with a look of curiosity, his dark eyebrows sloped downwards above his light eyes. I remained expressionless, not wanting to give him an invitation to speak to me.

"Okay, let's begin with our Five Question Fire Round." A chorus of groans played as the teacher pointed to his board, "the sound of excitement, excellent stuff.'

I allowed his voice to settle into the background as I began to write the date on the notepad, silently sighing at the sight of '2018'.

"Miss Garcia?" I looked up at the eyes staring at me as the teacher called my name again, "Let me guess, you went home last night and spent hours on Instatube and Yougram — or whatever it is you watch these days — instead of studying the work I gave you," he mocked as the room sniggered.

I sighed again, *I'm getting too old for this.*

"It's YouTube and Instagram and funnily, I spent my evening doing quite the opposite. Perhaps you would be so kind to please repeat the question for me?"

"Well, this should be interesting," he said, whilst I prayed it was a question I knew the answer to.

"In 1952, Britain declared a State of Emergency in which of her colonies because of the Mau Mau Rebels?" he questioned, leaning back onto his desk and crossing his arms, "Your fellow classmate, Jack, incorrectly answered Tanzania, as he thought it looked like the word Tarzan."

I sat up and placed the pen on the notepad, continuing to feel the eyes staring holes into me.

"Tanzania is incorrect, because it wasn't yet a country. It was formed as a sovereign state through the union of Tanganyika and Zanzibar." I began confidently, relishing every single dropped jaw and widened eye, including the teacher. "The correct answer is actually Kenya and the State of Emergency ended in 1960," I remembered reading about it in the news as though it was yesterday.

Don't worry, Effy, I got your back.

All eyes left me and jumped straight over to the teacher who laughed in disbelief. "That is actually the correct answer. Okay, who were the Mau Mau Rebels?" He watched me, waiting to see if my first answer was just a fluke.

The room was back on me.

"They were a militant movement that originated in the 1950's. They advocated resistance to British domination in Kenya." I said, sounding almost bored.

The teacher laughed once more, "Correct again, who knew you were listening to me all this time, Miss Garcia?"

I shrugged and put my head down, keeping my eyes on the date I had written. After satisfying the teacher with my answers, I was allowed to disappear into the background of the class, letting the noises fade away as the thoughts came tumbling in.

I had to lose Effy's dad before school ended. There was no way I could do this again. I didn't have the patience for the mean girls nor the jumped up teachers. The plan was to slip away after the lesson and hope that there was a local bus stop nearby.

The shrill of the class alarm sent the room into a sudden burst of movement.

"Remember, assignments are due back on Friday, absolutely no excuses and, Effy, can I see you for a minute?"

Were none of my plans going to come through today?

I slowly packed up my stuff catching Ayden looking over at me whilst his friends spoke around him. Now standing, it was obvious he played a sport or at least visited the gym often, from his broad shoulders and strong arms, displaying thick veins every time he moved his hands. He was the tallest of his friends too, though by only two or three inches at most. As he swung his bag over his shoulder, he gave me a curious smile, but instead of returning it, I looked elsewhere. I had no interest in entertaining any mind games from him.

"Effy?" the teacher spoke once the room finally emptied, "I didn't think I'd ever be saying this to you, but I was really impressed by you today. I've no idea what has brought it on, but I really hope it continues."

I nodded, ready for the day to be over with, "Sure, I'll try my best. Can I leave now?"

He nodded and pointed to the door, "See you next week, Effy."

I left the room and slid through the remaining few students trying to get to their next lesson or to their lockers. As I was about to turn the corner, I could hear Effy's name being mentioned.

"Is it just me or is Effy acting really strange today?" I tucked myself behind the corner, peeking to find Ayden, Brogan and their followers talking amongst each other.

"She's probably on her period." one the boys scoffed.

"Urgh, she is on something. She was being such a bitch earlier," Brogan replied, not taking her eyes away from her phone.

"No, but seriously, she isn't her normal self. When have you ever seen Effy wear *black*?" I watched as Ayden screwed up his face, "And the way she answered Mr. Pott's question. Since when was she smart?"

"What, are you worried she isn't interested in you anymore? Hey, she might even stop following you around like a lost puppy," one of the other girls teased.

"Why do you even care, you said you can't stand her — or is Jess right and you're worried you've just lost your back up?" Brogan looked up from her phone, looking more bothered than I imagine she would want to seem.

"No, trust me, I could get her any day. Just yesterday she texted me about twenty times begging that I go to her birthday party this weekend." Ayden smirked, "I just think she's a bit weird today, that's all."

I turned back, resting my head against the wall behind me and clenching my fists, feeling warmth rush to my cheeks as my heart began to race.

No, don't do it. Do not react. Let him think what he wants. We do not care. I repeat. We do not care.

"Okay, let's put your money where your mouth is. I bet you fifty quid that you can't get her to sleep with you on the night of her party." One of his friends suggested causing the rest of the group to look up from their phones and watch Ayden carefully.

"Deal!" he laughed and I could no longer help myself.

"Talk of the devil," one of his friends whispered as I watched the colour fade from Ayden's face.

"Hey. Ayden, right? So, I just overheard a bit of your conversation and I just wanted to make a few things clear, just so that we're all on the same page." His smirk was beginning to lose its confidence.

"Here's the thing, you've got about as much chance of 'getting with me' as you have of seeing those two leave Brogan's arse." I paused to look at the girls' faces before looking back at Ayden. "Now, I suggest that you hold onto that fifty quid as the only action you'll be getting this weekend is with your own hand. Do I make myself clear?"

He laughed anxiously, looking around at the faces of his friends, "Don't flatter yourself, Effy. Like I would really waste my time on someone as desperate as you." His friends began to laugh, stopping almost immediately as I shoved Ayden into the lockers.

"Wrong answer, Ayden. I said, do I make myself clear?" For a second, our eyes locked onto one another, and I noticed that, in the pool of green that made up his eyes, there were specks of onyx black.

"Whatever, now get off me." He cowered as he tried to shrug me off.

Dropping my arms, I leant into his body and whispered, "To think she thought you were worth her time... you're pathetic."

I finished and walked off, ignoring the whispered

insults directed at me and left the school with little care of who would see me. Climbing into my new car, I paused for a moment, catching my reflection in the side mirror. At that moment, in the pit of my stomach, I felt a twinge of guilt for Effy, just as I had for Taylor West. *School was tough.*

I didn't understand why Effy never stood up for herself. Why didn't she see her own potential and need the reassurance from others?

Feeling the rage boil through me, from a mixture of frustration of not yet fleeing the life of Effy, I began to hit the steering wheel, ignoring the pain that soon followed.

"Effy?" the voice startled me.

"Mr. Garcia!" I replied, kicking myself once I had realised what I'd said.

"Or perhaps just 'Dad'...?" He offered with pinched brows.

"Sorry...Dad. What are you doing outside?" I flustered.

"Effy, is everything okay? You really don't seem yourself today."

I thought about my answer carefully, giving myself some time to gather some composure. "Actually, you're right. I don't feel myself today. In fact, I don't think I'm feeling too well." I said frowning and placing a hand to my head, "Would you mind if I went straight home to get some rest?"

He paused for a moment and gave me a similar look that I had received from Ayden earlier in class. "Fine, but straight home and no going out tonight."

"Thanks, Dad." I smiled and started the engine.

"Effy, you know, if there is anything going on, you can talk to me?"

"I know. Thank you." He smiled at me before moving

out of the way and allowing me to reverse out of the car park.

Every now and again, I have what I call an obstreperous life, which is basically a nice way of saying problematic. It's not what I would usually label as a bad life, but it also wasn't great either. It was the kind of life that would prove to be a complete pain in the backside where no matter how long I had been doing all of this, I would spend the entire life dodging curveballs and jumping hurdles. I knew this was going to be Effy's life. Every plan I made seemed to have fallen apart and I was far too emotional than I liked. I had been Effy Garcia for less than 24 hours and I seemed more invested than I had in decades.

Not paying attention to anything but my own thoughts, I had subconsciously listened to the SatNav directions taking me back to Effy's home. Choosing to make the most out of being in the house alone, I made my way inside and went upstairs to the bedroom to pack a bag of everything I would need. It was as I pulled open the lid for a multi-coloured tin box that I found a folded up piece of paper labelled 'Dad'.

I already knew what it was before I had even opened it. I didn't know everything, but I did know the odds of Effy Garcia leaving a suicide note.

Dear Dad,

If you have found this then it means I went through with it. I'm sorry. I didn't want to leave you but I couldn't carry on any longer.

No matter what I did, I knew I was never going to be the person everyone wanted me to be or the person I wanted to be... I was never going to be enough.

Please don't be sad, just know that I am now at peace.
Tell Mum I'm sorry I let her down.
I love you so much, Dad.
Effy x

Normally, I found suicide notes before I knew anything about the body and nowadays, I wouldn't really take the time to find out the ins and outs, but this time was different because I had actually spent a few hours as Effy Garcia. I had seen how her life really was, so it was impossible for me not to feel sadness for her.

I continued to look through the box, finding pictures of both Effy and her dad smiling as though not a problem could ever exist in their worlds. Not only could you see how much Mr. Garcia cared for his daughter, but I felt it too. I felt his concern and worry each time he had looked at me that day. I didn't like to admit it, but I felt bad for him. Nobody deserved to lose their kid, especially not to suicide.

I closed the box and pushed it into the packed bag of clothes and toiletries before placing it in the back of the wardrobe, certain I was eventually going to regret my next choice, but going ahead with it anyway. I laid on the bed, stretched my arms and let myself catch up on the hours of sleep I had lost the previous night.

It was 11pm when I eventually woke up from the sounds of arguing coming from downstairs. It was mainly just a woman's voice shouting, but occasionally you could hear the low gruff of a man. I climbed out of the bed and quietly opened the door to listen.

"You just don't understand me anymore."

"You're right. I don't understand how someone can just give up on their family." Mr. Garcia spoke in a stern yet, calm manner.

"Given up? Why because I'm finally doing something I want to do? Where are you going? Don't you walk away from me!" she yelled back and I hurried back into my room.

"Elizabeth, enough!" he roared and just like that, she stopped.

I jumped back into bed, throwing the covers over me, but forgetting the light before the bedroom door opened.

"Effy?" Mr. Garcia called.

"Hi," I replied, awkwardly sitting up, hoping we wasn't about to have a father-daughter chat about his marital woes.

"I'm sorry about the noise." he said, sitting at the edge of the bed.

"It's not a problem."

He smiled weakly. "I heard about what happened in school today...with Ayden?"

My eyes fell to the bed covers as I muttered an apology.

"It's fine, if anything I'm relieved you aren't hanging around with those people anymore..." He paused for a moment, "but I won't lie, I found it very concerning when I heard you had gotten physical with him. What's going on, Effy?"

I looked up at his tired, worried face with eyes searching into mine as though that was where the answer lied.

"They're just horrible people and it was time for me to stick up for myself. I'm okay though, I promise." I smiled and it was genuine. "There is just one thing though, I really don't want to have this party on Saturday."

"But you have been looking forward to it for so long?" he answered, looking surprised.

I sighed and looked back down at the bed. "I know, but I just..." I had no valid reason except for the fact that if I was going to stick around a little longer as Effy, I really didn't want to celebrate another 17th birthday with people I didn't know or like.

"Look..." he said as he swung his arm around my shoulders, causing me to stiffen slightly, "Your mother is really stressed at the moment and you know how she loves these kinds of events. How about we just let her have the party and we do something another day, just you and me?" he offered with a smile.

Less than 24 hours as Effy Garcia and I knew I was already developing a soft spot for Mr. Garcia.

This was dangerous territory. This was going to make the end so much harder.

"Okay... Dad."

Chapter FOUR

I could have sworn that there was a time when standing up to bullies meant the end of being bullied. Sure, it wouldn't mean you'd become feared or have everyone begging to be your friend, but you were at least left alone. Apparently, this isn't the case in 2018 when standing up to bullies meant you just got picked on more.

I had spent the last two days being teased and mocked at every possible opportunity as Brogan and co. had started spreading rumours about me having an STI, whilst Ayden's friends threw stuff at my head whenever they had the opportunity. Ayden, on the other hand, had avoided me completely until Friday afternoon where it was announced we would be study partners for a history project. As the classroom alarm signalled the week was over, I breathed a sigh a relief.

"Effy, look..." Ayden's voice caused me to feel irritated immediately, "I'm not thrilled about working with you either, but I also don't want to fail History. So for the sake of our school grades, please can we just agree to be civil?"

I really didn't like Ayden. Not one little bit.

"You mean, you won't go around betting that you might get to sleep with me this weekend?" I mocked, "Or perhaps you'll get your minions to do that for you whilst they continue to spread rumours and throw stuff at me?"

Ayden sighed, "I said sorry and, for what it's worth, I have told the others to back off, but they won't listen to me."

I laughed whilst shaking my head, "No, you didn't say sorry and I'm sure you tried really hard to stop your friends..." I paused, not wanting to feed the building anger in the pit of my stomach, "Look, Ayden, I couldn't give a flying monkey about what you do and don't want. In fact, if you want to do this project then be my guest, because I won't be doing any of it. Now if you don't mind, I have a party to sort out." I sneered before walking off down the hall.

"Good for you, Effy, you don't care anymore, I hope that works out for you," Ayden called as his slow applause echoed through the empty hall.

The day of the party came sooner than I hoped and the house went from being a quiet house of three to several people running around setting up decorations and catering, all listening to the orders being barked by Effy's mother, Elizabeth. As I looked out of the window, I could see the large white marquee being filled with round tables and several shades of pink and gold decorations. I could guess this was more for Elizabeth than it was for Effy, but even so, it all seemed too over the top for a 17th birthday. I was thrilled to be missing out on the 18th.

Mr. Garcia had obviously noticed my lack of interest in the whole thing and would come upstairs to check on me every now and again, no doubt fearing I would run away—and I almost did when my birthday outfit arrived.

Of course, it was pink. Pale pink with pink roses and multi-coloured butterflies all on a mid-length 60's style dress where the skirt just kind of went...poof. Begrudgingly, I put on the dress and allowed the stylists to come in to fix my messy bun and tired-looking face. I, of course, demanded that no more shades of pink were to be added to my face nor would I wear any sort of flower or tiara in my hair. I was seventeen, not four.

Once satisfied with their work, the stylists left me alone and I sat on the window frame looking out of the window at the night sky beginning to creep in. People were already showing up in stunning dresses and black suits being greeted by Elizabeth and waiting staff with glasses of pink champagne. Elizabeth appeared to be in her element wearing a floor-length red gown and chatting with anyone that caught her eye. She was a strange woman. In the four days I had been Effy, I had barely seen her, always being told she was at work and then when I did see her, she would spend her time criticising me in subtle ways. I knew people like her couldn't help it, she was obviously struggling with getting older and spending a large chunk of her life being known as *just* a mother and wife. Elizabeth wanted to be seen, she wanted to be admired, but instead had a husband who was obviously devoted to his job and daughter, whilst her daughter grew up to be a beautiful young woman, reminding Elizabeth of her lost youth. So she broke free and tried to become someone for herself without realising how much she was pushing her family away. There would be a day where she would realise the results of her actions — probably when I left Effy's body — but it would all be too late, as it always was.

I continued to look out of the window spotting Brogan, Jessica and Naomi stepping out of a car, alongside a few of Ayden's friends.

"You'll eventually blow the house down with all your sighing." Mr. Garcia smiled, dressed in a grey suit and black tie. He walked over, sitting beside me as I continued to look outside.

"I see your 'friends' have shown up."

"Yep, and as you can tell I am thrilled," I replied, causing him to chuckle as I found myself looking to see if Ayden would also climb out of the car.

"There's a lot of people here, I'm sure it'll be easy to avoid them," he said, giving my knee a reassuring squeeze.

"Oh, don't you worry, they'll find me." I looked at his concerned face, "But I'll just ignore them." I quickly followed.

He stood up and offered me his hand, "Shall we go be the best trophy husband and daughter that there ever was?"

I softly laughed and gave him my hand, "Why not?"

The inside of the marquee was even more over the top than I had imagined with a ceiling filled with sparkling star-like lights and disco balls, amongst white strobe lights flashing across the otherwise dark room. Already people were spread across the dance floor and at the bar, chatting to each other over the DJ playing loud pop music. I stuck close to Mr. Garcia, wondering how I was going to play this one out. Except for a few faces from school, I had no idea who anyone was. At least with him by my side, I could rely on his reactions to the people that approached us.

"John! Fantastic, you could make it." He said excitedly and I tried to match his grin.

"Of course, how could I miss my favourite niece's birthday?" John replied, pulling me into his arms causing his scratchy black suit to irritate my arms.

"Thanks for coming, John." I smiled returning back to Mr. Garcia's side.

"I'm John now, am I? These kids grow up too fast, hey? How about we reminisce about the days when our kids were actual kids over a cold beer?" Mr. Garcia flashed me a strange look before walking off with John.

Great, I'm alone again!

Though, I wasn't for too long, because before I knew it, Brogan and co. were by my side.

I sighed loudly, quietly counting to five before turning to them, "Thank you for coming, girls. You all look *very* lovely." I put on my best fake smile.

"Well look at that, the bitch is no longer being a bitch." Jessica laughed.

One, two...

"Probably because she has realised she actually has no friends and that's why her party is filled with a bunch of her parent's friends. A little sad, doncha think?" Brogan mocked with a face full of spite.

Three, four, five...

"And frankly, your dress... it looks like a four-year-old just threw up its breakfast." she continued. To be fair, she had a point with that one. The dress was awful.

"Ok, well, I hope you have fun tonight, girls," I said with the false smile again as I began to walk off, only to be stopped by Brogan's hand on my arm.

"Where do you think you're going? To look for Ayden? Don't worry, I'll save you the bother, he isn't here. You aren't even worth a fifty quid bet." she laughed, tightening her grip around my arm.

I smiled and stepped into her so that my lips were a few centimetres from her ear, "I suggest you let go of my arm, Brogan." She hesitated for a moment before letting go and looking down at the red marks she had left.

"Please do not confuse my attempt of ignoring your insults for fear. See, the truth is, we all know you're the one that is upset about Ayden not being here tonight, because that's really the only reason why you've come." I smirked, watching as her eyes widened, "Of course, having the opportunity to mock me and my hideous dress is great and all, but you and I both know you didn't get all dressed up to just come and see me."

Brogan stood back whilst her friends waited for her to say something, but she didn't.

"I'm not afraid of you or your little girl gang, in fact, I have dealt with far worse and still come out as the winner. So please, drop this, Brogan, because believe me, I will come after you in ways you wouldn't expect. Now, as I said, have a nice evening girls." I smiled at her shocked face before walking off.

If I was right about the type of person Brogan was, I knew this wouldn't be the end of it and she would be plotting a plan to get me back, but for the rest of the night, I thought I would be okay.

A few hours into the party and with the help of some champagne, I began to feel relaxed, even dancing once or twice with Mr. Garcia and other random guests that I pretended to know. The party was in full-swing with most people on the dance floor, including Elizabeth, who seemed to be attached to anyone under the age of 20. Poor Mr. Garcia, I thought as I watched him pretend as though he couldn't see anything. It was then when I had forgotten about all the bad moments with Effy and let my guard down that I was reminded why I shouldn't.

"21 January 2018," I heard boom over the music, "Today was quite possibly the worst day of my life. I couldn't sleep at all tonight." I spun around recognising the words from Effy's diary straight away. There was Brogan beside the DJ reading from the diary as everyone quietened down to listen, excitedly as though something nice was about to be done.

"Where to start? My parents are driving me crazy with their constant arguing. At least Dad tries to hide it, but Mum loves to shout as loud as she can so that everyone, including the neighbours, can hear. I sometimes wish that she would just leave. I know that's what she really wants. Then Dad and I can just be happy without her constantly picking on us for every possible thing that isn't perfect about us." I tried to find Mr. Garcia's face in the crowd, but instead was greeted with hundreds of eyes staring at me.

"To make matters worse, I went into school today and Ayden ignored me the entire day. I don't understand why he hates me so much when I have done nothing wrong to him. I wish he saw me and thought I was pretty like Brogan. I wish I could tell him how much I..." She paused as an evil smile grew on her face, "Oh look, if it isn't the guest of honour himself." she shouted and everyone's eyes came off of me and followed my own.

Ayden stood still with a blank expression on his face but keeping his eyes on me.

"That's enough! Security, please escort this young lady out." I could hear Elizabeth's shrill.

I knew I should have felt embarrassment, but I didn't. One, they weren't my own words and two, this was all I needed to prove I had made the wrong decision in staying.

Effy didn't deserve this, nor did Mr. Garcia. But most importantly, I didn't deserve this.

Feeling everyone's eyes burning holes into me, I began to walk off, out of the marquee and into the house.

The little patience I had, along with the obvious case of stupidity, was long gone and no longer did I feel the need to stay and continue playing happy families with Mr. Garcia. I just wanted to live the rest of the year in peace and I knew the only way to do that was to leave.

I pushed opened Effy's parent's bedroom door and began to quickly sift through their cupboards. Finding Mr. Garcia's wallet, I paused trying to push through the guilt attempting to come to the surface.

This is not the time or place to consider your morals, Effy. It's time to go.

I grabbed the wallet and a few loose coins of change on their cabinet before going to Effy's room and stuffing it all in the bag I had hidden.

Grabbing clean clothes, I headed into the bathroom and began to get changed, cleaning the layers of makeup from my face. I tied up my hair before walking out of the room to find Mr. Garcia sitting on the bed with the bag beside him. His eyebrows hung just like his shoulders.

"What's going on, Effy? And before you tell me nothing again, don't."

I stood frozen to the spot, arms filled with toiletries.

"I refuse to believe that nothing has happened. In a matter of a day, you've gone from a sweet and harmless young girl to a thief that doesn't even seem to recognise half of her family." He pulled out his wallet from my bag as I continued to stay silent.

"You're not the Effy I know. She wouldn't run away from me and she certainly wouldn't steal from me."

"Yes, well, all this arguing is making me unhappy," I said silently cursing at myself for using such a cheap excuse.

"No, don't use that on me. We already had our plan — finish the school year and we'd leave."

Why on earth didn't Effy mention that in her diary?

"Something isn't right, Effy. You've called me Mr. Garcia at least four times, you're picking fights at school and tonight, you had no idea who John was, but seemed to know every single one of your mother's colleagues despite never having met them."

And this is why we don't ever stick around.

I slowly dropped the stuff in my arms onto the cabinet, knowing there was no way out of it. Even if I ran, he'd spend the next year trying to find me and — whilst I was brilliant at not being found — it seemed unfair to him.

I sat down on the bed next to him, keeping my gaze ahead, feeling the sweat from my palms beginning to dampen my trousers. I was going to tell the truth, and the last and only time I had done so, I spent the final few months of a lifetime in hell.

Are you sure you want to do this? Do we trust him? We don't even know his name yet.

"I have to tell you something..." I whispered, running through the plan in my head if it all went wrong.

Run. And keep running.

"Please, just let me try to understand, Effy. I can help you."

I nodded, "Okay, but you have to promise me that you'll listen to what I say with an open mind." I looked down at my fidgeting hands, "I've not told anyone this for a very long time and to say it ended terribly would be an understatement."

I could feel his eyes staring through me, "Yes, an open mind. You can trust me, Effy."

I took a deep breath, though it felt like no amount of air would soothe the weight on my chest.

"Mr. Garcia, what if I told you that you were right about me not being the Effy you know?"

"Well I would agree, you have changed."

"Yes, but what if that was because Effy wasn't here anymore and instead...I was."

"I don't understand." He frowned.

"Here's the thing. I'm not Effy. She died earlier this week — 28th of March to be exact — and when she left her body, I became her."

He took my hands into his, gently squeezing them, "Is this your way of telling me you're maturing and becoming a different person?"

"No..." I laughed softly, noticing his crossed brows. I removed my hands from his and held on to his arms, "Mr. Garcia, I am telling you that your daughter Effy is dead and I am a complete stranger who has taken over her body. I know this sounds absolutely insane, but I promise you, I'm telling the truth. That's why I didn't recognise a single face at the party, why I have been acting differently and why I don't even know your name."

I watched as his eyes scrunched up, creating one deep line growing across his forehead, "This might be the most preposterous thing I have ever heard..." he paused, looking at me with curious eyes as though if he looked hard enough, he would find the real me.

Good luck with that. Not even we know who we are.

"I know."

As I waited for him to say something more, I watched the confused look on his face fade into concern and then sadness. His eyes dropped to the floor as though weighed down by bags of stone.

"I don't know why, but for some very strange reason...I believe you." I looked at his serious face, waiting for a joke or laugh to follow, but it didn't.

Well, this is new.

"Ok... erm... thank you?" I fumbled, "But why? It's just that most people don't usually believe in a story like... this."

He nodded with what I could only describe as a broken smile — it was genuine, but hiding an immeasurable amount of grief, "Yes, but then I'm not most people and I know my..." He paused for a moment as his eyes glistened, "I knew my daughter very well. It's not been the same..."

I smiled, resisting the weird temptation to reach out and hug him, "Okay..."

We sat in silence for a moment, me not knowing what to do next and him not knowing what to ask first. I almost sighed with relief when he began to speak, ending the awkward silence.

"How is this all possible? I mean, how do you take over people's bodies?"

I shrugged, "I have no idea but I've been doing it for the last hundred years or so. Each year on the 29th of March, I wake up in a new body and die the following year on the 28th."

"A hundred years?!" he spluttered.

I nodded, "108 years to be exact."

"And do you enjoy it?"

"Wait a second..." I looked up at him, "I don't do this through choice. I don't just go around picking dead bodies to take over. It just happens. I'm basically trapped in a vicious, never ending cycle of lives."

"I'm sorry to hear that, it sounds miserable." He weakly smiled as I nodded in agreement.

"What's your name? Your real name?"

What is our real name?

It was a question that I had never been asked in any of my 108 lives. Sure, people had asked for the name of my body at the time, but no one had asked who I really was. Not that I could have given them an actual answer.

I looked up at his face and bit my lip, feeling a wave of sadness wash over me. Shaking my head gently, I shrugged my shoulders, "I have no idea. I know nothing about the real me, I don't even know if there *is* a real me. I first woke up in 1909 as John Baldon and this has been my life ever since."

Mr. Garcia smiled, "Don't worry, you can borrow 'Effy', she wouldn't have minded."

I returned his smile before resting my head on his shoulder, taking comfort in his warm smell as I gave in to the realisation of how comfortable I felt around him.

"What's your name, by the way?"

"Oh right, yes..." I felt his chest move as he laughed softly, "I'm Michael and your mother... sorry, Effy's mother is Elizabeth."

I nodded and smiled. The name Michael felt right, it felt familiar.

"Do you mind if I asked how Effy died? I knew she was upset and feeling low... please say it wasn't a suicide?" As I sat up and looked at the fear and desperation in his eyes, my heart grew heavy. I knew he deserved to know the truth, but I also knew it would completely break him and I didn't want to lose the first person to have believed me.

"It was an accident and it was instant. She didn't suffer," I said whilst remembering the red water and bloody knife that I had woken up to.

He relaxed for a moment, looking down at the floor.

"So, what do we do now? I can go if that would make things easier?" I asked in new territory.

"No, I want you to stay."

"What about your wife, Elizabeth?"

"Forget her, just pretend to be Effy, I can help you be better at it so that everything is easier for you, including school."

I sat back and looked up at him, "Mr. Garcia... Michael, I can stay and pretend to be Effy to your wife and anyone else, but I'm really sorry, I can't go back to school. I promised myself a long time ago that I wouldn't force myself to do anything that made me more miserable than I already am. What those girls did tonight won't stop there, they'll get worse."

"Okay, if you think it's best this way then I'll pull you from school."

"Thank you," I replied before hearing footsteps thumping up the stairs and heading straight for my room.

Elizabeth threw the door open and stood with a red face, "You!" She pointed at me, "I'll deal with you tomorrow, but you, we need to talk. Now!" She finished pointing at Michael before storming off once again.

"Duty calls." he smiled weakly as he stood up to walk to the door.

"Why is she mad at you? It was my fault."

"Yes, but when you have done something wrong, you are my daughter and only mine." He winked.

"I'm sorry."

He shook his head, "Nothing to be sorry for and thank you for being honest with me tonight."

"Thank you for believing me."

"Anytime."

I matched his smile, letting myself relax for a moment.

"Effy, just one thing and I know it's a big ask, but please... can you call me "Dad" for a while?" He smiled with glistening eyes, "I'm not sure I'm ready to stop hearing her say it yet."

I nodded, understanding completely, "Of course... Dad."

Chapter FIVE

I t had been a few months since I'd told Michael the truth and things had finally begun to settle. It took him some time to convince Elizabeth that taking me out of school wasn't as bad as she thought.

"She's not coping well enough. She's being bullied by those awful kids, having to listen to our disagreements whilst dealing with everything that comes with being a teenager. A gap year will do her good." Michael would say but after a few days, Elizabeth didn't even seem to care.

I'd spent the first few weeks being cautious, almost waiting for Michael to hand me over to the local mental institute, but he didn't and so I finally began to relax. Soon enough, we fell into a beautifully normal routine, something I hadn't experienced in a very long time. Both Elizabeth and Michael went off to work during the day, leaving me to do whatever I wanted until the evening came along and I would spend it with Michael.

It was strange not only having spare time and not having to spend it trying to stay hidden, but I also had a wealth of resources to truly do all that I wanted. I could get into my own car and drive wherever I liked without the fear of being recognised from a missing child poster. Gradually, I began to work through a to-do list that I had been mentally keeping for the past 108 years.

Each day, after waving Michael goodbye, I would

research the previous lives I had lived finding out what had happened next. Was the body found straight away or was I still considered missing? As I dived into the information, I started to note down where the bodies from London were now buried, finding that — out of the twenty-eight lives lived in London — thirteen were buried, thirteen were cremated and two were never found. Daniel Matthews was the most recent on the list, being the life I led in 2013 and was also buried about twenty-five minutes away. One afternoon, I climbed into the car and went to visit his grave. After some help from the friendly cemetery staff, I finally found the plot I was looking for.

A bare and aged wooden cross sat beside two graves with headstones and plenty of flowers.

Daniel Matthews - 29 March 1996 - 28 March 2013.

As I looked at his name inscribed onto the worn and smeared plaque, I remembered the day I woke up to a beating from a man that I later discovered was my new father. With my face in my hands already feeling the warm and sticky liquid dripping down my arms as my ribs were kicked over and over again, I panicked wanting to scream in fear and in agony. I bit my lip and continued to swallow the taste of blood and eventually, he stopped as the screams of a woman nearby distracted him. It was then that I realised I was in the middle of a poorly lit street. I kept my face covered, listening as the man sniffed and grunted a few obscenities before spitting on me and running away. I was taken to the hospital immediately and later diagnosed with four broken ribs, a broken leg, nose, jaw and finger. My wrist was fractured and so was my left eye socket. In total, I had ninety stitches across my body from my mouth to my ankles and had two operations to mend some of my broken bones. Doctors repeatedly told me that it was a miracle I was even conscious, let alone able to walk away after twelve weeks in the hospital with just memory loss. It was quite a scary thought to think that I had suffered all of that damage in the moments from waking up as Daniel. I wondered how much worse it was before the original Daniel had passed away and his deadly wounds had healed.

On the day before I was released from the hospital to the social services, I ran away and spent the rest of that life moving around each city of England. Eventually, I died, as usual, on the 28th of March, but my body wasn't discovered for several weeks. Whilst it was easier for me, it was a sad moment when I realised no one would come looking for the body I had left.

For some of my lifetimes, I occasionally wondered what life might have been like if they weren't involved in an accident or in the wrong place at the wrong time but there were some — like Daniel Matthews — that I knew that, even if they had survived that particular incident, there would always be another not too far away. People like Daniel were never going to get a happily-ever-after.

I walked over to the grave beside him, bending down to take a single white rose from the dozens of bouquets covering the freshly buried earth and leant it on Daniel's cross.

"Don't worry, Daniel, I'm sure your new neighbour wouldn't mind, she has plenty." I smiled.

"Effy...?"

I jumped before spinning around to find Ayden standing a few feet away from me.

It had been over two months since I had last seen his mortified face at the birthday party and aside from a few moments of curiosity, I hadn't thought of him or the rest of school since. I did my best to avoid any places where I might have found them and rarely left the house after 3pm, knowing that was when they were released from school. I didn't want anything to spoil the perfect situation I found myself in. When you have had to suffer with the 'Daniel's' in life, you realise just how good the 'Effy's' are.

"What are you doing here?" I asked, watching him walk over to me, carefully walking around each plot.

"I'm visiting my... I'm visiting someone. What are you doing here?" he questioned.

"Also visiting someone."

He looked around me and read out Daniel's name, "Who is Daniel Matthew?"

"My cousin." I quickly replied, hoping for dear life that Ayden knew nothing about Effy's family.

"Oh, I'm sorry to hear."

"Thanks." I replied, looking around at the cemetery filled with tombs, both old and new, "So, aren't you supposed to be at school?"

"I've finished for summer."

"Oh, right." I replied, only then remembering about the summer breaks.

"Are you coming back to school after summer?" he asked with a polite smile which disappeared once I replied.

"No."

Ayden looked at the ground as he gently played with a loose piece of dry mud with his foot, "You shouldn't let them get to you. Another year and you don't have to see them ever again."

Same could be said for Effy.

"And it's as easy as that, is it? Do you know what I had to go through, what Effy had to go through?" I stopped suddenly, hoping he wouldn't pick up on the fact that I had just referred to myself in the third person.

"Yes, but you are wasting your education on idiots. At least transfer to a different school."

"It's got nothing to do with you, Ayden. Now if you don't mind, I would like to be alone."

He sighed, looking a little hurt, "Sure Effy, whatever you say. Take care of yourself." he finished before walking off.

Feeling frustrated, I sat down on the dirt between Daniel and his new neighbour, Pat O'Brady. It was a strange thought to think I was at the grave of someone who had no idea who I was but I had spent almost a year being. With that said, despite living in his body, I didn't really know too much about him either. It was only through the police and social services did I find out my name and the facts of my family life. Two parents, fifteen charges of assault, ABH and theft between them and also eight children — five of which had been taken away.

When I first ran from the hospital, I became the local news story for a few months as the 'child beaten by his father had gone missing'. My new face was flashed on the TV as news anchors appealed I return home as posters were stuck up in shops and on trees but soon enough, the search stopped. People didn't really care anymore until a few weeks after my death and I made the local news once more. I was already in my next body, when it appeared on TV, "17 year old Daniel Matthews, who went missing from the hospital in 2013, after being beaten up by his father, Julian Matthews, was found dead this morning in an abandoned shed in Birmingham. Police have released a statement announcing the cause of death is unknown at this moment."

After a few hours had passed, I began to notice the sun beginning to settle. Standing up, I brushed the dirt from my bottom and said my goodbyes to Daniel. As I tried to remember the way back to the car, I spotted Ayden sitting by a headstone. Tempted to just continue to the exit, I stopped and walked over in his direction realising as I got closer that he was asleep with his head leant against the headstone.

Henry David West
  Father, Husband and Son
  Born 21 July 1975 - Died 19 June 2014

I re-read the black words inscribed on the white marble stone before looking back down at Ayden. He looked so peaceful that I almost felt bad for poking him to wake up.

"Effy?" he replied with confusion before looking around him.

"I noticed you had fallen asleep whilst I was on my way out."

"Oh..." he said, quickly getting to his feet, watching as my eyes ran across the stone once again.

"It's my dad." I looked up at his sad face and politely smiled, "it's four years today."

"I'm sorry," I said and meant it.

He nodded before we both watched a couple set some flowers down on a grave nearby.

"Don't you think it's funny how people leave flowers for

dead people even though they can't see them?" he spoke but continued to look at the couple.

"I don't think that the flowers are necessarily for the dead. I think it's more for the living. A way of making something that appears to be ugly look somewhat pretty."

"That's quite morbid." He looked up at me with a slight smile.

"So is dying," I replied and Ayden looked back at his dad's stone.

"Can I drive you home? That's if you didn't drive here yourself, obviously." I found myself asking, not sure what I was doing.

Ayden watched me carefully as though I was up to something before he smiled, "That would be helpful, thank you."

We walked to the car in complete silence, exchanging awkward smiles every now and again until he tried to apologise, "I know that what the others did was horrible and I swear, I tried to stop them, but once they have something in their heads, it's hard to get them to listen to anyone but themselves."

"To be completely honest, Ayden, you've not been a saint in all of this. I mean, who bets to sleep with someone?" I questioned but his gaze didn't move, "What kind of person does that? You were taking advantage of someone that cared about you." I finished as we reached the car. I didn't unlock the doors just in case the conversation went sour.

"I know that and I'm sorry. I swear!" he said, sounding almost desperate for me to believe him, "I wouldn't have ever tried to make you sleep with me, that's why I always blew hot and cold with you, because I didn't want you to think I liked you."

I laughed whilst shaking my head, "And you think that was doing me a favour? You made me miserable, leading me on as though I stood a chance with you and all the while, you were laughing behind my back, placing bets on my loyalty to you." I paused, feeling my blood begin to boil, "The problem with you, Ayden, is that you don't think about anyone else. It's just you that lives in that head of yours and that's pretty sad. You have no idea what your actions cause." I stopped and faced the empty road beside us, "We're never going to get along, so let's drop this." Ayden's gaze dropped to the floor as his forehead pinched together, "Do you still want me to drop you home?" I asked, softer this time.

"Do you want to know some really sad facts about me, Effy?" His voice was serious but if you listened carefully, you could hear it shake, "I fell asleep on my dad's stone earlier because I am so tired. I spent the entire night wandering around the area with nowhere to go, because my mum threw me out." This time, it was my turn to look down at the floor, "You're about to drive me to a home where I'm not even sure I will be welcome. Since my dad passed away, my mum has become an alcoholic. She lost her job and has slowly drank through any inheritance that was left to us. We've lost our house, our car and any chance of ever having a normal life." He paused just as his voice began to grow louder. He took a long sigh, "My older brothers and sister left me and my younger sister last year and ever since, I have been trying to take care of the flat we share, keep my mum from killing herself and my sister from being taken into care."

I held onto the car keys so tightly that it had began to leave a deep imprint against the skin of my hand.

"So tell me once more, Effy, how I don't think about

anyone else except for myself?" he finished, red in the face and avoiding eye contact.

I was speechless. Not only did I not expect to ever see Ayden again, but I didn't expect to find that beyond the ego-driven prick that I'd met previously, there was this Ayden. A broken Ayden.

"I'm sorry."

"So you've said."

I looked down at my hands still red from the key imprint, "No, I mean it. I should know better than to make assumptions about a person... you just haven't made it very easy on me."

"I get that."

I nodded knowing that somehow Ayden and I had just drawn the line over our differences.

"Can I still drop you home?" I asked opening the door as Ayden nodded and climbed in.

The first five or ten minutes were silent except for the radio playing quietly in the background. I wondered if the real Effy knew any of this about Ayden and if she had, would she still have killed herself.

"Does anyone know any of this at school? I asked, already certain I knew the answer.

"No. Why would they? I've seen how they bully you and you have the perfect life. How do you think they'll react to someone like me."

"Ayden, everyone has issues. No matter how big or small, everyone is dealing with something." He looked down before shifting his gaze out the window.

"Isn't it better to just be honest than continue to lie in order to fit in?"

"Don't judge me, Effy. We all remember what you did to Katie last year and all because you wanted to impress

Brogan. Nobody wants to be the person that no one likes, so you bend the truth and create a different you in order to protect yourself. You did the same when you sent that picture of Katie and I do it when I lead you on."

What picture?

As we pulled up outside of a grey and worn estate, I spotted a scruffy woman walking over to the car. As she reached the car, an overpowering smell of alcohol almost burnt the hair in my nose.

"Where the hell have you been?" she hissed, darting daggers over to me.

I could tell straight away that she was Ayden's mother. Not only because he had mentioned earlier she was an alcoholic, but because they had shared the same green eyes and pouty lips. It wasn't too difficult to imagine how beautiful she once was when you looked past the greasy brown hair and red, blotchy skin.

Ayden sighed, "Mum, I'll be there in a second."

She muttered something under her breath as she flashed me one last look and staggered off.

"I'm sorry," Ayden said.

"Don't worry." I smiled as he climbed out of the car, "I don't want this to seem as though I'm treating you like charity or anything like that, but I can ask my dad if he knows of any summer jobs to help you out. He's a good egg."

He remained still and I could tell he was contemplating whether or not to trust me, "Okay. I actually do like Mr. Garcia." he replied as I remembered Michael was also his teacher.

"Okay. I'll speak to him."

"Thanks, Effy." he said before walking up the stairs with dropped shoulders. He paused for a moment and turned back around to look at me. He smiled and as I smiled back, it felt like I was looking at a completely different person from the Ayden described in Effy's diary.

On the journey home, I wondered why Ayden had told me the truth. After everything that had happened between us, I should have been who he trusted least.

Once home, I did as promised and spoke with Michael who agreed to help find Ayden a job. I loved the way Michael wouldn't push for answers that I couldn't give and instead, reminded me that he was there if needed. I wondered sometimes if he had forgotten that I wasn't the real Effy, but I left it, not wanting to keep reminding him. We both knew that we had less than a year before Effy left for good, there was no need to dwell on it anymore than needed.

As expected, Michael had arranged a job for Ayden, but where and what it involved was not expected. One late morning, I woke by the unfamiliar noise of laughing from outside in the garden. I walked over to the window spotting Michael laughing at someone in a huge, yellow digging machine trying to get control of the large claw arm.

"I give up!" I heard the person chuckling before climbing out of the machine, "I'm sweating after that!" The voice spoke once again before beginning to pull off their grey top and turning around. I sucked in a sharp, short breath as I discovered it was Ayden standing in the garden, shirtless. I tried to tear my gaze away from his impeccable defined chest, worried he may spot me, but I knew it was too late as his lips grew into a knowing grin. I stepped away probably quicker than most comic book heroes and ran over to my bed, hiding under the cover.

"Okay, Effy, I'm starting to see the appeal now," I said aloud.

Once it had quietened down outside and there was no

58

sign of Ayden, I finally left my room and headed into the kitchen.

"Effy, I was just about to check on you. It's not like you to sleep in this late." Michael smiled, sitting beside Ayden.

"I've been awake for a while. I was just sorting some bits out." I said, cursing at myself for the reaction on my face as I spotted Ayden.

Get a grip, Effy. What is going on with you?

I pulled opened the fridge, scanning the contents about twenty times before settling on a leftover piece of cake, not actually wanting it.

"Do my eyes fail me or is Effy Garcia actually eating something bad?" Ayden mocked as Michael laughed, "I don't think I've ever seen you eat anything that wasn't green before."

"Yes, well she's a changed young woman." Michael smiled.

"So I'm beginning to notice..." I felt Ayden's eyes follow me.

"Okay, can we not make me feel bad for eating some cake, please?"

"Sorry!" They both said in unison, causing them to laugh again.

"What are you doing here, Ayden?" I interrupted.

"He's helping me. I've been wanting to install a pond in the back garden for some time now and thought why not during the summer holidays." Michael answered before giving me a wink. I wasn't sure if he actually did want a pond or if it was the only thing he could think of that might take a few weeks to do. Either way, he found a way to help Ayden.

"I'll probably be here every day, I hope that's okay,

Effy?" Ayden stood, walking in front of me to put his empty plate in the sink.

"Of course, no problem at all," I replied taking a few steps back.

"Cool." He smiled.

"Cool..."

We were so not cool.

"Well, as long as we are all done confirming our 'coolness', we better get back to work, Ayden." Michael laughed before walking off into the sunny garden.

"Effy, thanks again for this. I really appreciate it."

"It's my dad you should be thanking. All I did was ask him if he knew of any jobs, the rest was him."

"Thank you, anyway."

I smiled, "You better go before you're fired on your first day." I watched as he ran off into the garden, getting himself stuck into the job wondering how this would all play out.

After the first couple of weeks of Ayden working at the house, I began to get used to seeing him all the time, even Elizabeth stopped flirting with him and instead acted like a normal mum and occasionally invited him to a dinner she made. It was at one of those dinners that Elizabeth suggested that I begin driving Ayden home once he had finished for the day. Of course, in Elizabeth's eyes, having Ayden around meant that there was a possibility that her daughter could end up with the most popular boy in school and boost Effy's reputation. It was also a tactic to get me back into school.

"Well, it's getting late now. I think it's best you drive Ayden home, Effy." Elizabeth suggested as she threw her locks behind her shoulder.

"It's fine, I can drop him home." Michael jumped in after spotting the slight dread on my face."

"I can walk, honestly." Ayden offered but was ignored as Elizabeth stood up and looked down at Michael.

"Don't be silly. We bought her a brand new car so that she could do these things herself, Michael." Elizabeth rolled her eyes at Michael in a way that I had seen her do so with the house cleaner.

"Right, well... I guess I am driving you home, Ayden." I said breaking the awkward silence.

We left the house and climbed into the car, feeling just as awkward as we had done at the dining table.

"Music okay?" I asked politely as though I had just taken up a job as an Uber driver.

He nodded before returning his gaze to the window and just as I was about to allow the awkward silence to take over, Ayden turned to face me.

"I have been working at your house for almost two weeks now. How is it we can't seem to keep a conversation going for longer than a few seconds when we're alone?"

I laughed feeling a sense of relief as I shrugged my shoulders, "I was just thinking the same. I think it's because we don't really know each other." I answered truthfully.

"To be honest, I thought I knew you, but it turns out you are a completely different person to who I thought you were."

Little did he know.

"Just goes to show, you should never judge a book by its cover."

He nodded with a grin, "How about we play a game? Tell me something no one knows about you."

Good question.

With every life I had, things were different. Not just

who I was and what I looked like but the things I liked changed too. In one life, I loved Chinese takeaway and in another, I hated it - no matter how many times I tried. The only thing that was truly mine was my thoughts.

"I'm terrified of cats." he said before laughing, "I mean, I can be in a house with them, but the minute someone tries to get me to pet one or they climb near me, I'm frozen until it's gone." he admitted as I sat in a fit of giggles, noticing my grip of the steering wheel loosened.

"School football god, Ayden West, is scared of little cats." I mocked jokingly.

"Yeah, whatever." He rolled his eyes with flushed cheeks, "what about you?"

I looked up at the red light in front of me as I wondered if I should just lie - tell him something that was completely made up.

"Truthfully, my biggest secret coincides with my biggest fear..." I kept my eyes on the steady red light, "I'm scared I'll never figure out who I really am." I finished, admitting it for the first time out loud despite Ayden not having a clue at what I really meant.

"I wish most days that my mum would just get up and leave us and yet my biggest fear is that I will find her dead one day."

We stared at each other for a moment, feeling the most exposed and vulnerable we had ever been with one another.

"I can't believe how much I really hated you a few months ago and now look at us." I laughed, truly surprised at not only the change in our relationship but at myself for allowing someone new in. I'd regret it soon enough when it was time to go again and the next life wasn't nearly as good, but this felt worth it. It was nice to have Michael and Ayden around.

"Trust me, I was not a big fan of you either, especially that day you pushed me in front of my friends." he laughed.

"In my defence, you deserved it." I laughed back.

"What was it you said, 'do I make myself clear, Ayden?'" he impersonated me with a high pitched voice before laughing again and I couldn't help but join in.

"Oh, whatever. Shall I remind you of the dramatic applause you gave me when I said I wouldn't help you with the history project?"

"Hey, I failed that project because of you so my dramatic applause will be excused."

I smiled, "As you wish."

As we settled in the silence that had become comfortable, I thought of those first days when all I wanted to do was run, like I always did and yet, sitting in the car with Ayden, I was glad I hadn't.

"Do you think you'll come back to school after summer?" Ayden broke the silence.

I sighed and shook my head, remembering that once summer was over, half of my life as Effy would be too.

"What will you do? I don't want to argue with you, but I think it's a waste if you just do nothing."

I smiled, "Maybe I'll get a job, who knows? I'm trying this new thing of just taking each day as it comes."

Ayden nodded, "It's going to be strange going from seeing you everyday to hardly ever."

I laughed, "I'm sorry, but does going back to school mean forgetting where I live?"

"No, but it'll be harder." He flashed me a weak grin before looking out of his window, avoiding me.

"Even if I did go back, which I *am* not, we wouldn't have hung out anyway. You still have the same friends,

Ayden. The same friends that caused me to leave in the first place."

"But I could at least try to talk to them."

"You already did, remember? And it didn't work then so why would it work now?" I shook my head, not prepared for another argument, "Look, let's not get into this again, I'm happy with my decision. We can just be summer friends." I smiled and nudged him but only getting another weak smile.

I didn't return straight home after dropping off Ayden that night, instead, I drove around London, reminiscing all the other times I had seen the same monuments through different eyes and in many different decades. I couldn't explain it, but I always felt at home in London, as though it was where I was supposed to be. It was the same feeling I got when being in the body of a female as opposed to the initial awkwardness I felt in a man's body. I remember the first time I woke in John Baldon's body. I was shocked to find myself as a man and immediately wished I was a woman. The same happened when I woke the following year as Catherine Young in Australia. Whilst I was more comfortable being a girl, I felt out of place by being one in Australia.

It was strange because, living as John, I had no memory of seeing anything before and yet, I recognised the various monuments in London, knowing where a particular place was or how to get somewhere. I didn't know if it was possible that I might have lived before John Baldon but I knew that if I had, I was definitely a girl and London was home.

"You and Ayden seem to be getting on well lately." Michael pointed out once I got back home and found him sitting in the living room eating ice cream and watching a film.

"Yeah, he isn't the worst friend to have," I replied, keeping my eyes on the TV.

"Have you told him... you know, about... you?" he asked as though I was the one that might have needed reminding.

"No."

"Do you think you might? I think you could trust him."

"No." I snapped, "and I'd appreciate it if you didn't say anything either."

"Effy, I told you, you can trust me. I just think you can trust Ayden too."

I sighed, "What's the point? After summer, he'll go back to school and I'll go back to being forgotten."

"Okay, I won't push this, it's up to you, but I think you are underestimating how important your friendship is to Ayden," Michael replied before walking out of the room, leaving me with my thoughts.

I trusted Ayden. He knew things that no one else did, but the things he knew about me were realistic, if not obvious. Telling him the truth about me seemed impossible. Just because Michael believed me, didn't mean anyone else would. I had been down that path and didn't want to see someone who I cared about think I was crazy. And even if he did, believe me, our friendship was based on me being Effy — and I wasn't really Effy.

What did it matter anyway, his visits would soon stop.

It's not worth the risk.

The next few days, I was purposely distant to Ayden, spending as much time as I could out of the house and making Michael drop Ayden home. I couldn't see a point in continuing a friendship with him that would end shortly. It was simply a waste of my time when I could be doing so many other things.

Instead of hanging out with Ayden and Michael, I began to spend the days visiting places that I'd been in previous lives, finding the little name carvings I would leave behind in each life. At first, I did it to prove to myself I wasn't going insane and was, in fact, returning every year as a new person, but then it became a tradition. Some had long gone with the change in buildings or worn away with time, but some still existed. On the side of a pillar of the old Albert Bridge were the faint initials of Simon Hart, my life in 1991. On the brick walls of Charing Cross station hid the initials of Nellie Hawkins, my life in 1949 and on a bench in Hyde Park were the initials of Lottie Day from 1965.

Once tired, I would check the time and head back home once I knew Ayden would have been taken home. However, on one night, whilst researching another lifetime, Ayden walked into my room without warning.

"Why are you avoiding me?" he demanded, his hair all ruffled to one side with bits of paint on his face. Due to the hot summer we were having, Ayden looked as though he has been holidaying in the Caribbean and not the back garden.

"I'm not and thanks for knocking," I said closing the laptop.

"Oh stop with this cold shoulder crap, Effy, it's getting boring now."

"Then leave," I replied, not looking up once but instead busying my hands with some paperwork.

"We are friends, Effy. I've told you things that I have never said to anyone else." He frowned at me.

"No, we are not. You work for my dad and I was just trying to be nice to you."

"Don't give me that. You don't get to decide if and when

we're friends. We are friends and that's final." The corners of his mouth twisted slightly as he continued, "Now, when you've stopped being an idiot, I'll be in your car waiting to be driven home." he said, grabbing my car keys from the side and walking off, leaving me staring at the opened door trying not to look impressed.

I lightly chuckled before sliding my feet into some boots and going downstairs where Michael was sat on the sofa with a smirk.

"Not a word," I said and he smiled whilst zipping his mouth shut.

Ayden was leaning on the car looking down at his phone before noticing me walking towards him. The corner of his mouth raised upwards creating a playful grin as I rolled my eyes, "Keys." I demanded, doing my best to not give in to his infectious laugh.

"Glad to have you back on board, Miss Garcia." he said once we were both in the car.

"I'm just being a nice person and dropping you home." I kept my eyes on the road, but could feel his smile all over me.

"Sure you are." he said, resting his head on the headrest behind him, "Boy oh boy, am I glad we are friends again, your dad's jokes were actually starting to become funny."

"We are not friends."

"Yes, we are. You need me as much as I need you so stop being a big ol' baby and get over it." he teased, "Look, I know I said that it would be hard to stay friends when I went back to school but truthfully, I was just trying to use it as a tactic to convince you to come back to school. Whether you're there or not, we will always be pals." He nudged me gently.

I laughed out loud, "You thought you could use withdrawing our friendship as a tactic to get me to go to school?" I continued to laugh, "How big is your ego?"

"Deny it all you like, but I know how much you enjoy having me around and it's not like you have a queue of friends outside your house, so I'd be nice to the one you do have if I were you."

"And I wouldn't go around mocking the one decent friend you have if I were you."

"Touché." He laughed and I gently chuckled.

"Talking of school, don't you start again next week?"

Ayden nodded with a sigh, "Yep, tomorrow is the last day of working with your dad. We finally get to fill the bad boy up!" he finished excitedly.

"You know, we have never spoken about what you want to do when you finish school?"

He sighed again, dropping any sign of a smile, "The dream is to play football professionally, mainly so I could afford to look after my sister and put mum in rehab, but realistically, I'll probably take the first job that comes along."

"What about uni?"

"And leave Kira with my mum? No chance. Anyway, what about you?"

I shrugged, "I don't know."

Truthfully, I never allowed myself to think about it, as it would only be a form of torture, thinking about a future that I would never have.

"Well whatever you do, I know it'll be amazing." He smiled as though he actually believed it, "Hey do you mind if we stop here so I can grab some treats for Kira? I'm a rich man these days." he joked as he pulled some loose coins out from his pocket as we walked off into the shop when Brogan appeared in front of us.

"Well, look who it is." she laughed, "I thought you might have run away for good after that horrendous party."

"Nice to see you too, Brogan, I see you haven't changed," I replied.

"Why the hell would I change? This is what normal looks like, sweetie. Perhaps you should go back home and look it up instead of chasing Ayden around like a lost puppy. He isn't interested in you, don't you get it?" she spat and I turned to Ayden, waiting to see if he would step in and tell her to back off, but he didn't. He stayed silent with eyes full of apologies.

I smiled, ignoring the twinge in my chest before turning to Brogan, "There's that jealousy again, Brogan. You really should work on that and if 'normal' is you, then I'd rather be literally anything else. And as for you..." I said, turning to Ayden, who was standing still with no sign of life, "friends have each other's backs. That's why we are *not* friends."

I walked out of the shop and climbed into the car, ignoring Brogan's cackle and as I drove home, I gave little care to traffic lights or other cars honking their horns at me. I ignored Elizabeth when she called my name as I walked past her to my bedroom, locking the door behind me and climbed into my bed, laying still, in fear that if I didn't I might cry.

Chapter SIX

In 1957, I fell in love with a boy named Walter Valentine. In the almost 50 years before I became Lila Henry, I had dated and fooled around with a few boys, but I had never been in love.

Walter Valentine was the 18-year-old that everyone in Brooklyn knew or wanted to know and if you didn't know him, then you definitely would have heard of his family. His dad was Robert Valentine who had helped the Brooklyn Dodgers to success after the Second World War whilst his mum was the lead 'Sally' from the girl group, The Four Sally's. Of course, this led to him and his younger sister, Betty, to be the most popular kids in high school and at first, I couldn't stand either of them. It wasn't until after summer when Betty and I became juniors and were made to join the dance committee that we became friends. Within a few weeks, we were inseparable and I had become almost as popular as Betty. Don't get me wrong, people knew of Lila before I came along and she was liked by most, but we had gone from being a backup for our own school dance to having seniors inviting us to their final dance. That didn't matter though, because I had a feeling a certain senior would eventually ask me.

Being Betty's closest friend meant frequent sleepovers and invitations to dinners and parties. It also meant I was on Walter's radar. Whilst I liked Betty, I still wasn't sure on

Walter, who acted as though he was entitled to anything. Sure, he was ridiculously good looking with slicked-back brown hair and a mischievous grin that broke hearts aplenty. He was also the only guy in school who could look stupidly cool in his black leather jacket and black sunglasses. But he still treated people terribly in order to get his way. He would date numerous girls at the same time and drop them when he pleased, unconcerned at how he broke their hearts. He could get whatever he wanted, whenever he wanted it. At least he did until I came along.

With most seniors being too frightened of Walter to ask Betty out, I was the next best thing and I was catching all their attention. Hearing of the failed attempts to get me to accept their dance invitations, it wasn't long before Walter joined in on the mission, except he didn't ask. His tactic was to get me to ask him. Little did he know he was up against the queen of patience.

At first, it was just a game for me, a way to teach Walter a lesson that he couldn't always get what he wanted. I'd play along with his flirtatious teasing and the cheeky winks he'd give me in the school halls. When that didn't have me falling all over him, he stepped up and began to give me his full attention at school. He'd whistle at me instead of wink so that everyone could hear and would often swing his arm around my shoulders when we were all together. I used to love watching the amused confusion that would spread across his face when he wouldn't get the reaction he had hoped for.

It was during his next plan that I realised that some-where down the line I had started to like him. He stopped giving me any attention and instead, began pouring it over others. I knew what he was doing straight away and would politely smile back when he flashed me a nonchalant grin, but I couldn't deny the twangs of jealousy I would get when he'd put his arm around another girl or whistle at another. This continued for about a week when I overheard a conversation between Walter and Betty. I stood outside of her room and listened intently as my name was mentioned.

"Is she dating anyone?"

"Why do you want to know?" Betty asked the very same question on my lips.

"I asked first."

"No, she isn't seeing anyone." Betty sighed.

"So, she genuinely doesn't like me." he said before laughing, but it was a confused laugh.

"What are you talking about, Walter? Do you like Lila?"

"What does it matter, she doesn't like me." he said and walked out of the room, pausing as he saw me standing outside, "You're definitely something, Lila Henry." he chuckled before walking off into his own bedroom.

I wondered to myself over the next few days if I should just admit to him that I liked him, but I couldn't allow myself to give in so easily, so I began to tease him, making an effort to get his attention, just as he had done to me. I started with the winks and cute smiles and then moved on to whistles and leaning on his arms. I could see it was amusing him just as it had with me, but it was as I was beginning to flirt with other seniors that I started to realise that it was starting to irritate him. One afternoon, he had finally had enough and pulled me into an empty classroom.

"What are you playing at, Lila Henry?" he said as I leant against the wall behind me.

"What are you talking about?" I replied with my best innocent face.

He stepped forward, leaning one hand against the wall above me.

"I've spent the last six weeks trying to get your attention and you've not so much as batted an eyelid my way and now..." he stopped and smiled as though he had just worked it all out, "and now you're teaching me a lesson." He shook his head.

I smiled looking into his endless dark brown eyes.

"You are something, Lila Henry."

"So you've said."

"Are you going to the dance?" he asked as I rolled my eyes and ducked underneath his arm, "this is all it's about, right? You being the guy that I say yes to."

He smirked and walked over to me, standing so close that our noses almost touched.

"Then we won't go."

My heart was beating so loud that I was sure he could hear it too. I could feel my palms beginning to grow clammy, but I stood still with an unrevealing smile across my lips.

"We?"

He nodded, "Yeah, we."

As he finished speaking, he lowered his lips onto mine and my heart skipped several beats. We spent the next few months as one of those couples that everyone moaned about but secretly wished they were part of. When March arrived, I was absolutely heartbroken that I had to leave him, spending the final days deciding whether to tell him the truth. I didn't, of course, deciding instead that if I found myself in another girl's body, I'd try to find him and make him fall in love with me again.

That didn't happen, though.

As the clock struck midnight, I woke and discovered I was a boy and also living in Manhattan, not far from Walter. Straight away, I went to Lila's house and watched as he was told the news.

I left shortly after and never went back, promising I'd never put myself through that pain again.

As I wiped away the fallen tear from Effy's cheek, I realised I had broken my promise, but this time it wasn't for someone that cared about me like Walter Valentine. It was for a coward named Ayden West.

It had been a few weeks since the incident with Ayden and Brogan and I knew he'd be back at school, pretending to be someone else again.

He had messaged me twice, asking me to hear out his apologies, before I blocked his number and told Michael that I wouldn't be accepting any calls from him. Michael was, of course, as understanding as ever, leaving me to tell him what had happened when I was ready and willing. When I eventually did, he smiled and took me in his arms, only saying one thing on the matter, "Let's hope his fear doesn't become his regret."

During the month of October, things had become more stressful. Elizabeth was asked to host her boss and his wife, who were visiting from the states, for dinner and whilst to most this would have been seen as an honour and a fantastic opportunity, Michael warned me that Elizabeth wouldn't see that way.

"That man! If he thinks I don't know what he is up to then he has another thing coming." she'd mutter far too often.

Michael also warned me of the chaos the house would

become. The week before the dinner, Elizabeth had a cleaner come in twice a day whilst hiring a temporary housekeeper. If she so much as saw a speck of dust in the air, she'd demand they begin hoovering and dusting once again. Meanwhile, Michael and I were ordered to eat out every night and I was told to either stay in my room or go out. Two days before the dinner, we were all sent for new haircuts, Michael also had to have his little ash coloured stubble beard removed, but the day of the dinner was by far the worst. We had a chef prepping the kitchen, cleaners literally hoovering the air and waiting staff arranging the dining room, all whilst Elizabeth barked orders. Of course, Michael and I stayed well away until she came storming upstairs and demanded to know why we weren't ready at 2pm for a dinner at 6pm.

"It would do you some good if you matured a little, Ophelia. You act so childishly sometimes." she tutted at me before spinning on her heel and walking away.

"Ignore her." Michael rolled his eyes and not for the first time, I could see exactly why Effy struggled with her mother. But that particular day, Elizabeth was at her worst. It started that afternoon with little insults, such as me being lazy or messy, but as time went on, she became more stressed and the insults would be laced with poison.

"Goodness me, that skirt looks absolutely awful on you. You've put on so much weight...Where you got that hair from, I don't know, it's certainly not mine...It's such a shame you took your father's genes over mine, you'd have been much prettier."

I stood back in complete shock, wondering how she thought it was acceptable to speak to her own daughter like that. The truth was, I looked great and she and I both knew it. The skirt she said looked awful was a black A-line skirt that went over the knee and I wore it with a lace cream long sleeved top and black strappy heels that made the ball of my foot burn every time I was stood. A red lipstick was put on my lips and my apparent lion's mane hung loosely around my face.

I smiled at her insults but slowly, they began to bother me. Dinner seemed to have gone perfectly with both Mr. and Mrs. Tonkin's laughing and smiling. I was the model daughter, replying to questions and creating intelligent conversations.

"Michael, Elizabeth, what an absolute wonder your daughter is. You must be very proud." Mrs. Tonkin spoke delicately as they said their goodbyes.

"Agreed, there is always a place at the company for you, Ophelia. We could do with some fresh and young talent." Mr. Tonkin added.

Michael and I breathed a sigh of relief as the night was finally over and had gone smoothly, but the feeling wasn't unanimous and when Michael left to buy us some treats from the shop, Elizabeth fell off her witches' broom.

"How dare you embarrass me like that?" she shouted, causing me to almost choke on leftover potatoes.

I couldn't help but laugh in disbelief, "Are you kidding me? How on earth did I embarrass you?"

"Oh, you know what you did..." she snarled with a wagging finger as she walked closer to me.

"You are going to have to enlighten me on this one, because I honestly have no idea what you're talking about. I was friendly and polite. They even pointed out how great I was... oh..." I stopped, realising what it was that provoked her, "I was the perfect daughter this evening, so perfect that I took all the attention away from you. Mr. Tonkin said the company needed fresh and young talent, of which you're neither and you're *jealous*." I spoke now on my feet, standing directly in front of her.

It was when you were inches away that you saw past the expensive makeup and face creams and found the *real* Elizabeth. A woman so scared of her own reflection, because it held a truth she didn't want to know.

Then, she hit me hard in the face with her hand, knocking me off my feet, causing me to land with a thud. I held my cheek, as it stung with a feeling of fire before I looked up at Elizabeth's face, watching as it went from anger to shock. I pulled myself up, letting go of my burning cheek before slowly shaking my head, "No wonder she committed suicide. There's just no pleasing you." I spoke before hearing a creak from the floorboards behind me. I closed my eyes and prayed with all my might that no one was there.

"Effy?"

I turned around and found Michael standing by the door with a plastic bag full of sweets. The hearty smile that would light up anyone's face was gone, along with the glimmer of hope that usually filled his eyes. It was as though the Michael I had become fond of was gone and a shell of a man stood in his place. My insides tightened as I watched his mouth about to move. I felt sick.

"You lied to me?"

"What's going on?" Elizabeth spoke, but no one replied. My eyes stayed with Michael.

"I'm sorry." It was all I could muster up as I fought hard not to cry.

He nodded and slowly put the bag on the floor before walking over to me. My heart raced and I could feel my hands trembling. I hadn't been this scared in a very long time.

"I'm going to believe that there's a very good reason why you lied to me and I'm sure everything will be fine tomorrow, but..." he paused and I could see his red eyes beginning the same fight I was having, "not tonight." he whispered before walking off upstairs.

My heart sunk as I tried to swallow the lump in my throat.

"Can someone please tell me what the hell is going on?"

Elizabeth's voice went straight through me as I wiped my damp face and turned to her, "Oh, shut up."

I grabbed my car keys and stormed out of the house, wanting to get as far away as possible.

Hours later, I was sat in a quiet booth in a bar with my head resting on the table, watching the cool drops of water roll down my glass whilst quietly reciting the name of every life I had lived. As soon as I thought of Michael or Ayden, I started from the beginning.

"John Baldon, Catherine Young, Mary O'Sullivan, Robert Friend, Abraham Giselle... ."

Michael...

I sighed feeling the heaviness of the alcohol weighing me down. Every limb felt as though it was being held down by concrete. I couldn't move, not even when I heard someone slide into the booth and clear their throat.

"Effy?"

"Go away." I slurred, recognising the voice immediately but keeping my head on the table.

"What are you doing here?"

"Swimming." I rolled my eyes, "Surely you of all people know what people do in bars." I stopped immediately and quickly forced myself up to look at Ayden. "I'm sorry." I sighed, "I shouldn't have said that. You should just leave me alone. I'm best alone that way I can never hurt anyone and no one can hurt me."

"Effy, what's going on? This isn't like you."

I laughed and leant my head back against the wall, looking up at the yellow smoke-stained ceiling, "Probably because I'm not Effy. I'm not John either. I'm also not Catherine, I'm not Mary or Robert. I'm not anyone. I don't exist and yet I keep coming back." I laughed before sighing loudly.

"I'm sorry, Effy. I don't understand."

"Don't worry, no one does... except for Michael. He understood, and what did I do? I lied to him and now he hates me."

"I'm sure he'll forgive you."

I sat up, eyes so tired they burned, "You're right, he will, but I don't deserve it. And you know, I wonder why this keeps happening to me, why I keep waking up every year. It's because I'm a bad person."

"I think you've had too much to drink, Effy."

"You should stop thinking then." I slurred, watching him slide out of the booth and stand by the edge of my seat, "Come on, I'm taking you home."

"No, it's fine. My car is outside."

"You can't drive in this state, Effy."

I pushed him out of the way as I rose to my feet, feeling as though my legs no longer belonged to me, "Yes, I can, because I can't die, remember? Oh, wait..." I said covering my mouth and laughing, "I shouldn't have told you that. Oh well, now you know, I can't die! Not until the clock strikes midnight on 28 March." Ayden walked behind me, carefully leading me out of the bar where people were now watching my antics.

"I wonder where I'll go next time? You know, everyone

goes on about what way is the worst to die — being burnt alive, drowning or being stabbed, but it's none of them. Yeah, I know first-hand how much they hurt, but there is something that hurts so much more. Do you know what that is?" I looked up at Ayden with his arm around me trying to hold me up as he looked for a taxi.

"Being all alone when you die." I sighed, "Do you know how many times I've died alone, Ayden?"

"Never Effy, because you're alive." he answered frustratedly.

"Wrong!" I shouted in a childlike way, "108 times." I looked down at the floor and bit my lip hard, "108 times I have died in different bodies and in different countries, but always alone." My eyes began to sting, "Nobody knows what the true meaning of loneliness really is until you are forced to take your final breaths with no one telling you that you're going to be okay, that you'll be missed or that they love you. You'd think I would be used to it by now, but instead it just gets harder."

"Look, I'm going to get you home. You'll feel better once you have slept this off." Ayden said once he had successfully flagged down a black taxi.

"I have nowhere to go. I'm not welcome at the house." I said as we climbed into the car.

"Where to, mate?" The driver called out and Ayden looked down at me with a look of concern.

"Ballymore Estate, please." he replied as I rested my head on his shoulder, convincing myself that the taxi was not actually spinning. It wasn't long before we arrived on the poorly lit street.

"Where are we?" I asked as we climbed out of the car and Ayden paid the driver.

"My house." he replied as I recognised the door that I

had seen him walk towards months ago. The street was quiet and not as harsh to the eye when the lights were off as though the darkness hid its flaws.

"You can stay at mine tonight, but you have to promise me you'll be quiet. If my mum hears you..." He stopped and I could see he was regretting his decision already.

"I don't have to stay here." I held onto his arm as he looked down at me.

"No, I want you to."

My stomach fluttered for a moment.

"Let's go." he muttered and I followed behind him as we walked into the quiet house. I was surprised that even in the darkness, the inside looked nothing like how I had imagined. Where I had expected to see worn carpets, peeling walls and mess everywhere, there was rich wood flooring with fluffy rugs, decorated walls with family photos and the house smelt of lavender, and lemon bleach.

We walked upstairs and into Ayden's bedroom.

"My mum's room is downstairs, so we should be okay to whisper." he said, switching on the light to reveal a clean and spacious room. Again, not what I had expected. The walls were painted white with frames of football tops scattered amongst the shelves filled with trophies and medals. In the corner of the room was a double bed with a laptop opened and opposite the bed was a large chest of drawers with a TV.

"I think this might be the tidiest bedroom I have ever seen that belonged to a boy," I said, trying to read the engravings on his trophies but seeing two of each letter.

"Yeah, well, that's another thing about my mum, she's got OCD. She's had it for as long as I can remember, but since drinking, it's gotten much worse." I nodded finding a picture on a shelf of Ayden and his family. His mother looked just as I had imagined her before the alcohol; a warm smile and big, bright eyes. Beside her stood a tall man with dark hair, he wasn't looking at the camera, but instead at the little blonde girl in his arms. It was the same look I had become used to receiving from Michael.

"Is this your dad?" I asked, realising Ayden stood behind me.

"Yeah, it was a few months after my sister was born." he replied, taking the photo from my hand and putting it back on the shelf.

"He looks like a lovely dad." I smiled.

"He was." Ayden replied, walking to his chest of drawers and pulling out some clothes, "Here is a pair of shorts and a T-shirt, get changed." he ordered and so I did. I pushed down my skirt carefully, feeling the cold air hit the tops of my legs.

"Effy! I meant in the bathroom." Ayden covered his eyes and turned his back to me.

I couldn't help but giggle as I took the clean clothes from his hands and replaced them with my own.

"Are you decent?" he asked as I pulled on the grey T-shirt that hung on me like it would a hanger.

"Yes."

"Good, now get into the bed." he said, pulling the covers down.

"Where are you going?" I climbed into the bed, watching him walk over to the door.

"I am going to sleep in my sister's room." he said with careful eyes.

"Ok." I replied, feeling a little disappointed, "Do you think maybe you could stay with me... until I fall asleep?" I whispered.

He took a moment to reply as though he wasn't sure if

he wanted to before turning off the light, walking over to the bed and lying beside me.

I laid back with a relieved sigh and scooted closer to him, feeling the warmth from his body. As I looked at him staring up at the ceiling, I couldn't tell if it was the alcohol or his musky smell that made me feel dizzy. My heart raced and I could hear my breath shake.

"You should try to get some sleep." he spoke, stiff as a board.

"How did you find me tonight?" I whispered.

"I was actually looking for my mum, but then my neighbour called letting me know she had just walked in when I heard you calling out these random names."

"You could have just left me."

"No, I couldn't have."

I rolled onto my back, moving away from his warmth as I allowed myself, for just a moment, to believe he cared about me until I remembered the night with Brogan.

"How's Brogan?"

He sighed and turned his head to look at me, "Effy, I'm sorry, I know I should've defended you."

"No, I can defend myself. I just wanted to know you were there for me." I said, turning over so that my back faced him, not wanting him to see my face anymore.

"I know and I am now. I don't care who knows that we're friends anymore. I'll tell everyone if that's what I need to do for you to realise that." He stopped and I couldn't help but look back to him to see what he was doing.

"I don't want to lose you, Effy. You're an okay friend." He smiled weakly.

I returned his smile, "You're not a very good friend, but it's okay, we can work on it." I turned back to face him again, and laid my head on his chest, listening to his heartbeat, feeling the rise of his chest each time he breathed and eventually, I slowly drifted off to sleep.

The buzzing of a phone caused me to wake, but I didn't open my eyes, instead, I allowed myself to go back to sleep once the phone had stopped. It wasn't until a raging headache began to pound its way through every part of my skull that I became aware of my surroundings. A persistent bright glow demanded I open my eyes as I began to smell a mixture of lemon bleach and a warm, musky scent. It wasn't a familiar smell, not something I had become used to in the Garcia home. It wasn't until I felt something move behind me and the sensation of someone's warm breath on my neck that I realised I wasn't home.

I opened my eyes to the bright sunshine peering onto me through the gaps in the blinds and carefully looked back at Ayden who was still asleep, cradled into the shape of my body. It was strange to see him looking so peaceful as the seemingly permanent frown he wore was gone. As I listened to the faint sounds of his deep breaths, I wondered what he dreamt of. Whether he ever got relief from all the worrying he did about his mum and sister, or his fear that someone would one day discover who Ayden West really was.

The buzzing noise started again and I slowly edged myself away from Ayden, carefully lifting his arm off my waist before slipping out of the bed. I pulled the phone out of my bag and found fifty-six missed calls and twice as many text messages, all from Michael. Just like those waves that knock you at least ten feet, the memories of the night before crashed into me and sent me flying. I cringed as I remembered getting undressed in front of Ayden and almost stopped breathing when I recalled being at the bar and telling Ayden the truth.

I need to get out of here.

Whilst convincing myself that he would just suspect I was drunk, I pulled on my skirt and grabbed my shoes and phone before tiptoeing out of his room. As I headed for the stairs, I looked at the family pictures on the walls, all at least a few years old, but looking at them now, you'd think it was a different lifetime. I continued looking at the photos until I reached the last step and was greeted by Ayden's mum, clearing her throat with a frown.

"I didn't realise we had guests." she spoke much differently from the slurs I had previously witnessed, she also smelt of the lemon bleach that had lingered in the air.

"I'm sorry. Ayden was just helping me out, I had nowhere to go." I spluttered, feeling the heat in my cheeks smother my face.

"Effy, is it?"

"Yes, Ms. West." I nodded, rooted to the bottom step.

"Please, Quinn is fine. Orange juice? I usually find it helps with the hangover." Her voice followed her into another room.

I didn't dare say no despite really wanting to leave and speak with Michael. Instead, I followed her into the modern but small kitchen with each wall covered in either a cupboard, utensil or spice rack, hiding the off-white colour.

Quinn pulled open the fridge and I noticed the paintings that had been drawn by Ayden's sister that all seemed to be family portraits that included their dad.

"Sit." she ordered as she placed the cold orange juice on the table before sitting in front of me with her own drink.

"It's just water." she answered my questioning eyes.

I opened my mouth to say something, apologise or deny anything she thought I might have thought, but not a single word fell out of my mouth.

"I'm not stupid, I know what you think of me."

I shook my head, "No, not at all." I lied.

"You're not a very good liar, Effy." She made me feel on edge, the same way Ayden did with suspecting eyes that seemed to look through the body I wore.

"I'm sorry." I apologised looking down at the floating bits in the juice, "Despite how it may seem, I actually might understand the position you are in more than you think."

She watched me curiously, but also allowing me to go on, "I can see you still have pride in your home and you love your family which means somewhere past the need to drown yourself, there is someone who is stuck in a cycle wanting to get out."

Quinn began to chew on her top lip, already raw from earlier chewing, "Every morning I wake up promising myself that I'll not drink that day, that I'll give it all up, but then I remember why I started. I know it sounds stupid, but I wasn't made to live this life alone. I'm not one of these independent women you see doing it all on their own. I need someone to lean on. I'm not strong enough by myself." She swished her glass around as though it was actually whiskey and ice instead of water. I reached out and held on to her hand, stopping her from moving the glass as her eyes looked up at mine.

"I think that it takes a lot of strength to keep going when all you want to do is give up."

She returned my weak smile, "Even if that was true, I fear it's too little too late. My kids don't see me as their mum anymore, at least not the mum I was or they want."

I smiled, "There's a whole lot of cliches coming out of me this morning, but as long as you're still here, you still have time." Quinn squeezed my hand as I replayed the sentence over in my head.

"You're a very smart girl, Effy. Your parents must be

very proud of you. Ayden has said how close you are to your dad."

I thought of Michael at home, searching for me despite me lying to him and though Quinn had time to change things, I didn't.

"I am and if you don't mind, I need to see him."

She walked me to the front door and gave my arm a gentle squeeze, "I'm glad you're friends with my Ayden. He won't like me saying this, but I've seen a difference in him this summer and I'm pretty certain it's because of you." She finished with a smile before waving me off to find a taxi.

I winced as I slid my sore feet into the heels and checked my phone for the time. It was 6.05am and the streets were bare except for the occasional car driving past or drunken body staggering its way home. No matter the year or lifetime, I always found that in the early morning hours of a Sunday you could see London at its stillest.

Not managing to find a taxi, I pulled off my heels, deciding that the risk of treading into something amongst the debris on the streets would be far less painful than another step in the horrid shoes.

I had spent many lifetimes walking the London streets, some years it was even what I found to be home and maybe it was my immortality, but I always felt safe, always finding where I needed to be. I smiled as I was greeted by the memories of a former life.

On paper, it should have been one of the more rubbish

lives, what with being a homeless teen in the 60's. I woke up in a shivering frenzy, wiping the dampness from my icy nose. Sitting up, I found myself on a pile of stacked cardboard boxes with a once white, but now grey sheet covering me. The room was poorly lit with only a tiny bit of light forcing its way through the ripped cardboard stuck up at the windows. Even with no light, I could still make out the room. It wasn't very big and not very well looked after with its peeling walls and stained carpets.

It wasn't difficult to work out that I was, in fact, homeless and, having been homeless before, I wasn't instantly worried. As with all the homeless teens I had been, I had no way of knowing who I was or even my own name so I would usually make one up.

In this particular life, I became Doris Monroe, for reasons I'm sure are obvious and for the first few months, I used my previous experiences to survive. What was once dumped furniture on the rundown corners of the East End became the new features in my condemned flat in an abandoned block. It was empty except for myself and Mr. Tripper, who lived several floors above me and kept very much to himself.

As well as scouring the streets for unwanted treasure, I also investigated the other flats. Most were trashed from earlier rummaging, but I was able to find a worn mattress, some cooking utensils and clothes that would be helpful once I had cleaned them. I would steal the other necessities I needed, such as food and soap until I was given a waitress job, earning £4 a week and two hot meals a day, ending my need to steal. It was here that I met The Samson Brothers, Bobby and Frankie. They were the nephews of my boss, Jonny, and the same two boys that the majority of the East End were touting as the next Beatles. It wasn't long before I became friends with them, despite my attempts to keep them away, but they were far too infectious and it never took long before they had you smiling. Eventually, I began to attend the small shows they'd perform in around the smaller London clubs, watching as the crowd, mainly filled with young girls, would swoon over the boy's cheeky grins and slick black hair. They loved the attention of course, and I would usually leave them after the show to the flocks of girls desperate to get to know them.

Despite being friends, Bobby and Frankie didn't know much about me and never pushed when I tried to change the subject or fed them something we all knew to be lies. That was until Bobby followed me home one night, after a local show. No one, of course, knew where I lived and no one had even asked, though I wouldn't have told the truth even if they did, but that night, without noticing, Bobby followed me into the block. He crept up the stairs behind me and a few seconds after closing the door, he knocked. In the six months of living in the flat, not one single person knocked on my door, not even Mr. Tripper, so my first thought was that it must have been trouble. Immediately, I grabbed the knife I had stolen from the restaurant one evening, once Jonny began to trust me to lock up, and prepared myself.

The door knocked again as I remained still, cursing at myself for becoming too relaxed and not checking around me when walking into the flat.

"Dee, I know you're in there."

I sighed and mumbled a few swear words as I recognised the voice and the nickname that only The Samson brothers called me.

I raced over to the window and wondered if I should jump. It was about thirty-foot high from the floor and though surviving wouldn't be the problem, it was whether I could make it to the bottom and still run off.

"I've got all night, Dee, you'll have to come out eventually," Bobby called through the door. I took another look out the window and sighed.

Hiding the knife, I walked to the door and began to unbolt the several locks. As I opened the door, I was greeted by a curious looking Bobby with his hands tucked into his black pea coat with the collar up, just like all the boys wore it. He pulled off his matching black visor hat and peeked around me and the door.

"What is this place, Dee?"

"Why are you following me?" I replied.

He lifted his left bushy brow before slipping past me into the flat, "I asked first. Are you living here?"

I was honest that night and admitted to Bobby my current situation, skipping the whole, 'I'm not actually Doris Monroe'. It was then that he revealed he had an older sister, Susie, that ran away several years before and had never returned. After an hour of me politely declining Bobby's offer of staying with his family, I finally gave in and began to pack up my few possessions.

"Why are you helping me, Bobby?" I asked as I watched him peering through the window at the twinkling lights of London.

"Because I'd like to think that this is what people do when they find a lost soul." He smiled before taking the bag from my hands and leading me away from the first six months of my life as Doris Monroe.

The next six were the exact opposite. Soon after moving in with the boys and their parents, they were discovered at one of their local shows by someone from the same label as

The Beach Boys. In a whirlwind, they were signed up and made to work on their first single which was a song that Bobby had written years before. It wasn't long before the song was released and the boys became a hit in the UK, just as the residents of the East End always said. With their first album ready to go, I was ready to wave them off as they were lined up to begin a UK tour to find that Bobby had convinced their manager to find me a job that allowed me to join them and so I became the secretary of The Samson Brothers.

After the UK tour, we were flown over to Germany where the boys had become huge before flying to France and then finally to the States. We couldn't believe that in six months, the boys had gone from being two brothers performing in seedy East End nightclubs to becoming an international hit, being uttered in the same breath as the famous bands that already existed. I became the envy of millions as the boys openly spoke about me in interviews, hailing me as their good luck charm and making a track, titled 'Dee'. I nearly lost track of time when I realised my birthday was only a couple of days away.

"What's going on? You've got that serious face on where you get a wrinkle between your brows." Bobby teased as I sat him down one evening.

"Bobby, I need to go," I said, not wanting to leave, but also not wanting them to find me when the day came.

"What do you mean? Where?"

"Home. This has been incredible, Bobby. Like a dream, but it's not my dream, it's yours and Frankie's. I think it's time for me to see what's next for me." I smiled, feeling the lump in my throat form bigger.

"There's nothing I can say to change your mind?" he asked and I shook my head.

"Okay." he replied sadly before I reached out and hugged him tightly.

"Thank you..." I whispered, "for finding my lost soul."

I left that day and died a couple days later, never seeing The Samson Brothers again except on the TV and I would always beam with pride as the boys became more and more successful each year.

I returned to the street, finding my car parked half on the curb and a yellow ticket under the windscreen wiper. Throwing the heels and the ticket on the back seat, I pulled my phone out of my bag and began to read the messages from Michael.

"Where are you? Please respond to me....I'm very worried, Effy. Come home....Just let me know you're safe."

Much like Bobby, Michael never challenged my answers to his questions, he always understood and reminded often that he cared, even though I wasn't the real Effy. He found my lost soul.

I threw the phone onto the seat and answered my own unasked question, "I'm going home."

Chapter SEVEN

I pulled into the drive and sat for a moment, watching as the blinds of Effy's bedroom moved. I slowly climbed out of the car, preparing myself for the shrill of Elizabeth's voice and the disappointment from Michael, but it was only Michael that arrived at the door with a face of relief. I didn't move but instead waited as he began to walk over to me before pulling me into his warm body. Slowly, I hugged him back and it was a few minutes before he carefully let me go.

"I'm glad you came back." he said as he scanned me over, as if he was looking for any harm that might have come to me.

As we entered the house, I noticed Elizabeth in the kitchen cleaning as she called out 'good morning.'

"I told her that you had stayed at Ayden's," Michael said from beside me.

"How did you know I did?" I asked but able to answer my own question.

"Ayden messaged me. The problem is, I had no idea if you'd return."

We didn't speak again about me running away or the truth about how Effy died, instead we carried on as normal, as though the evening had never happened.

Later that night, once I had settled back into the life of

Effy, I received a text from Ayden. I felt the earlier embarrassment as his name flashed on the screen.

Ayden West: So you spoke to my mum.
    Effy Garcia: I did.
    Ayden West: Well, you've set her off on attempt 9000 to get sober.
    Effy Garcia: Well at least she's still trying.
    Ayden West: It's hard to take it seriously when you've seen it all before.
    Effy Garcia: Again, at least she's trying.
    Ayden West: Right... are we arguing?
    Effy Garcia: No.

I watched as the grey dots appeared on the screen and disappeared several times until my phone began to vibrate with Ayden's name flashing for me to answer. A flutter of butterflies strummed through my stomach, as my thumb hovered over the 'answer' button. As the call came to an end, I sighed with a mixture of annoyance at myself and relief that I didn't answer. The annoyance began to outweigh the relief once I realised that Ayden wouldn't call again, nor would he text.

I slumped back on the pillow and slowly felt the tiredness begin to drown out all my worries, replacing them with the relief of sleep and being back home. Later, I woke from the noise of a faint tapping. As my eyes adjusted to the darkness, I realised it wasn't coming from the door but the opposite side of the room. I climbed out of the bed and opened the patio-styled windows to a small iron balcony. I stepped out into the cool air and found Ayden beneath me with a smile and an awkward wave.

"What are you doing here?" I whispered.

"Were you asleep?" he asked instead.

"Of course I was, it's the middle of the night."

He looked at his watch and back up at me with a smirk, "It's 9.34pm, hardly the middle of the night."

I looked behind me, back into the room for the clock to see if he was telling the truth and it had been about thirty minutes since I had last texted him.

Feeling embarrassed, I looked back down to him, "What do you want?"

"Well..." he said slowly as he pulled out what looked like a white handkerchief tied to a pen. "I wanted to surrender in person to whatever fight we are apparently having." he finished waving the makeshift flag.

I looked away so he couldn't see me laugh, "We aren't fighting." I said once I had forced the smile away from my face, replacing it with a blank expression. I knew exactly why I was pushing him away and it wasn't just the fact that I had shamefully undressed in front of him but that I knew him well enough to know that the minute I entertained his company, he would begin quizzing me on what I had revealed to him the night before.

"I think we are, but like I said..." he shook the handkerchief again, "I surrender." He flashed his smirk once again, "So can we please be friends again and you come down here instead of you continuing to throw me daggers."

As he stood grinning up at me, it was hard to not replicate his smile, but instead I sighed and walked back into my bedroom. Sat in the dark with only the light from the moon shining through the opened windows, I looked around at the tidy bedroom and spotted my shoes in the corner by the door. Like a loud alarm with no off switch, the worries of Ayden quizzing me rang loud as the memories of a bad lifetime came flooding in. Michael was the second person I had ever told my secret and I was extremely lucky that he handled it so well. I couldn't test that luck and risk it with Ayden, but I also knew it would be hard to stay away from him. This life was proving to be more of a challenge when it came to thinking with my head and not any other internal organs.

Laying back onto the bed, I swallowed a mouthful of guilt as I imagined Ayden outside waiting for me.

Even if you don't see him tonight, you'll have to see him eventually.

"So, I'll just continue to ignore him," I replied to the guilt.

But he'll just keep coming back, you know he won't listen.

"Then I'll make him listen."

"You'll make who listen?" As the voice spoke, I shot to my feet to find Ayden at the door, "And why are you sitting in the dark?" he spoke again, searching for the light.

"Leave it off." I ordered, "What are you doing here?"

"Suit yourself, and surrendering, remember?" He waved his flag gently.

"I mean in my bedroom? I said I didn't want to talk."

As he closed the door behind him and set the flag down, he sat down on the bed, "No, what you actually did was walk back into this room and for a second I thought you were coming down, but obviously you weren't. So, if the mountain won't go to Mohammed..." he quietly cut off and flashed a smile that one could mistake for nervousness.

Not knowing what to say, I walked over to the window instead, looking up at the almost full moon.

"So are you going tell me what I did? As far as I'm aware, it's nothing and actually, if anything, you should want to keep me as a friend even more so now."

As my heart stopped beating for a moment, my head spun so quickly that I had almost given myself whiplash.

"What do you mean even more so now?" I asked trying to stay as unfazed as possible, but not doing the best job.

He chuckled, "Well, some might say that I was your hero yesterday, coming to your rescue and taking care of you."

Relief washed over me like a cold breeze causing me to shiver, "Oh, yes. Hero — ha!"

"Hmm." Ayden's brows pinched in the centre as he stared at me curiously.

"What?" With my hands fidgeting and heart rate erratic, I scanned his face as he replied.

"Well, it's just that last night, you were talking about how you weren't the real Effy and how you would die on your birthday, just as you did every year..."

As he continued, I tried to think of anything to say to stop his current thought process, but no words came. Instead, I just stared at him, wondering if he would really figure it out.

"And at first, I thought it was nothing but you being drunk. And then last night, I couldn't help but think about what you had said and your reaction just then...well...just call it the cherry on the cake."

I turned back to the balcony, feeling the tug in my stomach and the burning in my cheeks, "I think it's time that you left, Ayden."

"No..." I felt his hand on my arm as he replied, "You're hiding something."

I looked up at his face, highlighted only by the glow of

the moon as though he was in a black and white film. His eyes were fixed on me, scanning my face for a response. Though he knew I was hiding something, I knew he didn't know what it was. No one ever did. Only storytellers could possibly imagine my secret. Every now and again, I would find a life that would lead me to find a special person, the kind that would stay with me forever. I already had Michael this time, so I didn't have any hope that I would have a second person in one lifetime, but I realised there and then, that I did and it was time for me to tell Ayden the truth.

"Ayden, I need to tell you a story..."

In 1923, I woke as Nancy Duggan in Cork, Ireland. She looked as striking as her accent with long black hair and icy blue eyes. As a barmaid for her father's busy pub, I met Cuan O'Calen. He was older by a few years and had fast become a regular at the pub. Nothing was done slowly in this lifetime and within a week, I was head over heels in love with Cuan. We were inseparable and fast forward a few months, Cuan was on a bended knee asking for my hand. In the blindness of it all, I tried to forget about my repeated fate and when the reminders wouldn't cease, I found myself visiting a gypsy one dark night. She held my palm and told me she felt a curse upon me, it was none like she had ever seen before.

Naively believing her ability, I told her the truth and she promised she had lifted the curse and I could marry Cuan without fear that my life would end soon.

The next morning, whilst asleep and dreaming of my future, fists pounded against the front door, "Miss Duggan, open up now!"

Grabbing my dressing robe and not finding Cuan in bed beside me, I called his name.

"Miss Duggan, if you do not open, we shall have to break down the door." The fists thumped on the door once again.

Unable to find Cuan and terrified that something had happened to him, I took a deep breath and opened the door.

Quickly, I was tackled to the ground as two large men cuffed my hands before facing me towards Cuan who stood in the corner.

"Is this the woman you described?" one of the men asked causing my heart to shatter into pieces as Cuan nodded and allowed the men to carry me into the ambulance. It was only days later when I was sat in a cell in an asylum that I discovered that the gypsy had told Cuan I had an illness which doctors later diagnosed as Schizophrenia. For months, I suffered from various types of cruel treatments knowing that it would be months before I would eventually die, but nothing hurt more than the memory of Cuan allowing the men to take me away.

Before Michael, that was the only time I ever revealed my secret and I was about to do it all over again.

"Say something..." I pleaded as I watched Ayden register what I had just told him, "Do you believe me?"

He rubbed his eyes and leant on his hand before looking at me with a careful glance, "If you say it's true then I believe you... it's just so..."

"Insane?" I finished with a nervous smile.

Ayden's face remained still, his eyes still locked onto mine, "I knew something wasn't right but this is... who else knows?"

"Just Michael."

He nodded before standing up from the bed and moving to the window where he looked out of the window, "You said you only go into the bodies of those that had died... how did the real Effy die?"

To be honest, I didn't want to tell him the truth. I wanted to lie so that it wouldn't hurt him, but I knew he needed to know. I had learned the hard way with Michael.

"She committed suicide," I whispered.

He didn't say a word and he didn't need to as I watched his shoulders slump and his hands leave the railing and cover his face.

"Because of me?" he spoke quietly.

"It wasn't just you. Brogan and the girls and even her mother all played a huge part."

He exhaled loudly before excusing himself to the bathroom where I listened to him throw up. After a few minutes, he returned back to the room with a face as white as ash. As he sat beside me, I noticed his hands shaking.

"Does Michael know how she died?"

I nodded slowly, "Yes, but he doesn't know why and you can't tell him, Ayden".

"But he should know I'm to blame..."

"No..." I grabbed his hand tightly, "and you aren't the only one to blame. A lot of people played a part in her death, Ayden."

He smiled weakly as his eyes glistened, "But I could have stopped things. I knew she was being treated badly by the girls and I kept messing her around. I could have just stopped things. She killed herself..."

I took hold of his cold face and forced him to look at me, "Yes, you could have done things differently, but you aren't solely to blame. She was unhappy Ayden, because of school, because of home...because of a lot of things. Whilst I don't condone how you treated her, you have to remember that you are under a lot of stress yourself and you're not a bad person... okay?"

His eyes stayed on mine, looking past me as though someone was behind me before falling to the ground as he nodded.

"Ayden, Michael has suffered enough. He already has to live with the fact that his only daughter is gone and that a stranger is now living in her body. Soon enough, he'll have to say goodbye to her for real. He has had enough."

Ayden nodded before lying back on the bed, "So you'll leave for good in March?"

I sighed as I laid beside him and replying yes.

"What happens?"

"I usually have time to prepare and I make sure I'm somewhere I can be found unless I don't want to be found." I sighed, "It usually begins about an hour before where I begin to gradually feel weaker and weaker until I can no longer stand and I have to lie down. I try to sleep, but most of the time I can't and so I just lie there as my heart begins to slow and my eyes grow heavy and the next thing I know, I wake in another body."

"And it happens every year?" He turned his head to me, but I kept my eyes on the ceiling.

"Since 1909."

"And you can't die before?"

"No, I have tried everything. I can be hurt, but can never die. At least not until 28th March."

"So, who are you really?"

A heaviness in my chest grew as my eyes began to sting, "The all-important question..." I smiled as I faced him, "I don't know. The first person I became was John Baldon, but I started his life just as I have everyone else. I know there was someone before that, but I have no memory of them."

"So you could actually be a boy?" he smiled and I couldn't help but return it.

"I guess I could, but I don't think I am. When I first became John, I had no idea what I was doing, but then I was a girl the following life and I felt more comfortable."

I watched as Ayden looked up at the ceiling, his eyes darting around looking for something that wasn't there.

"Do you think it's a curse?"

I softly chuckled, "It certainly feels like one, but whatever it is; curse, hex, illness, magic, there's nothing to fix it."

"But when did you last try? Surely you're more likely to find a cure in this day and age?" Ayden sat up suddenly with more energy in his voice.

I slowly sat up and sighed, "It was several years ago, but Ayden, I had been looking for ninety years before I finally gave up. I've accepted that there is no cure. Please don't go getting yourself caught up in trying to find a way to help me. You'll only waste your time." His face sunk a little before he nodded and laid back down.

"Just doesn't seem fair."

"You're telling me."

A cool breeze brushed against my bare arms as my eyes adjusted to the bright sky piercing into the room from the opened window. We were currently having one of those late summers in October where, for two weeks, everyone in London would forget that Winter was fast approaching and keep out their summer wardrobes, complaining about the heat.

It had been a few weeks since I told Ayden the truth and to say things had changed between us was an under-statement. Occasionally, he would text or call to see how I was and blame a busy school schedule for his unavailability. Michael would vouch for him, explaining how it was all prep for their final year, but I wasn't stupid, nor was this my first lifetime. My situation confused *me* at the best of times, let alone others, and I knew that it was just too much for Ayden to be okay with. As long as he didn't say anything, everything would be fine.

I started the day like I had most. I climbed out of bed mid-morning, pushed open any windows and took myself to the shower where I would waste the best part of an hour. Eventually, once dressed, I'd make my way downstairs as the clocks neared noon and eat the lunch that Michael left me in the fridge. Michael wouldn't usually be home before 4pm and Elizabeth would return later in the evening most nights. Some might say I was being wasteful, spending my days lazing around, but patience wasn't much of a friend to me anymore and unless I had to do something, I simply enjoyed the rest.

This particular day was different, though. As I left my room to find my lunch, I was instead greeted by Michael and Ayden sat at the table.

"Effy!" Ayden said with a grin on his face.

"Ayden," I replied in a nonchalant tone as I looked for my lunch.

"It's not in there today, Effy. I thought we could have lunch together." Michael spoke.

"Aren't you supposed to be at work?"

"It's the weekend." Ayden chuckled as I sat opposite him at the table.

"Why are you in such a good mood? And since when did you become the best of friends with my dad? Don't you have a reputation to uphold?"

Ayden ignored the look that I shot him and instead pulled out a worn A4 envelope.

"Well, I've got something to share with you but first, I need you to promise you will just listen before you jump on your 'I know everything' horse." His smile dropped slightly, replaced with a more serious look as I nodded curiously.

"I decided to do some research after you told me the truth and — "

"No, Ayden." I interrupted and stood up from my chair, "I do not want anyone doing any research into anything. I've been around for 108 years, don't you think I would have found help by now?"

"You said yourself that you haven't checked in the last fifteen years." Ayden stood and called after me as I went to leave the kitchen. "Effy, times have changed. We are not Cuan or anyone else, we just want to help."

I stopped and turned to face him, now standing beside Michael.

"And I guess you're on his side?" I asked.

Michael shook his head and walked over to me, placing his hands on my shoulders giving a gentle squeeze, "No Effy, we are both on your side. You know the last thing I would do is let any harm come your way, but I have checked his research and I really think you should at least listen to what he has to say."

As Michael finished talking, I looked into his eyes filled with so much warmth.

"And if I say no, then it's no?"

"One hundred percent! I promise I will drop it if you don't want to do anything more with it." Ayden spoke from behind Michael.

I sighed and tried to ignore the memories of Nancy Duggan, "Okay, show me."

Michael and I followed Ayden back to the table and watched as he pulled out the documents from the envelope, spreading them in front of him.

"Ok, so to start, I did a few searches on the internet on 'body jumping' and 'taking over people's bodies' etcetera, but I found nothing useful." As Ayden continued, I watched as he separated some papers and handed them both to Michael and me.

"But then I thought about it for a few days and realised it was your soul or spirit...whatever you want to call it... it was that that was jumping into bodies. So I started researching soul jumping and it's a thing!"

"What do you mean, 'it's a thing'? You mean, there are others?"

Surely, it was impossible that I hadn't crossed paths with one before.

"Yes. Well, not exactly. You see, there are tons of forums on this sort of stuff. They all talk about leaving the body whilst dreaming and taking over another body, but it's always when they are sleeping and never longer than a few hours but past all that, I found a website belonging to a spiritual group called The Shal Vida.

"I'm not interested in a cult, Ayden."

"They are not a cult and you promised to listen..."

I raised my hands in submission and let him carry on, already sure that we would never speak of this again after he had finished.

Sure, nowadays people had places online to post about their lucid dreams that felt as though they were in another body, but at the end of the day, that was all it was, a lucid dream that they'd eventually wake up from.

"Anyway, so I researched them and I guess they follow this type of spiritual religion, but something they talk about is 'anima ferventis' which means..."

"Soul jumper." I finished as I began to read the paper Ayden had given me.

"Yes, in Latin. How did you know that?"

"108 years, you learn a language or two," I replied, scanning the page.

"Right, well anyway, the Shal Vida's believe that souls can enter other bodies sometimes, but on very rare occasions they can control bodies for long periods of time. Coincidence or not, it all sounds very similar, so I reached out to them."

"You did what?" I yelled, throwing the paper on to the table.

"I reached out to them using a random email address off of a proxy to hide my IP address. There's no way of tracking it to me."

I sighed loudly, "This isn't your place to be doing any of this."

"Effy, just listen to him." Michael nudged me.

Ayden waited for a few seconds, perhaps to see if I would interrupt again, before pulling out another piece of paper. This one was a print out of an email.

"They replied yesterday... here."

I hesitated for a second as to whether I wanted to read the words on the paper Ayden offered to me before taking it and beginning to read it aloud.

"Dear Mr Ronaldo..." I stopped and looked up at Ayden who displayed a small smirk on his lips, "doesn't sound conspicuous at all."

"It was about 4am when I sent the email and the first name that came to mind."

I rolled my eyes and continued to read.

"Thank you for your email of which I found most interesting and passed on to my mother, Aniya. My mother has been practising Shal Vidas since birth and is a direct descendant of Shaya Myronsol. In her 77 years, she's become a great healer of souls and has helped many individuals with their lost souls.

When hearing your story, I knew it was something she would find great interest in. My mother has dealt with many temporary soul losses and whilst she's been told stories of permanent losses, she's never heard of a case like yours. It's for that reason that she would like to see you and see if she can help locate your true self.

We look forward to hearing from you."

I stopped reading and placed the letter on the table.

"So?" Ayden waited with excited eyes.

"I appreciate the time you've put into this, Ayden, but this is as far as it goes."

Ayden's face dropped as I rose to my feet and walked off into the garden.

As unappreciative as I seemed, I liked that Ayden

wanted to help, but what was the point? No one could help me. I was trapped in this endless life and no spiritual healer would change that.

"Effy?" Michael spoke softly as he sat beside me on the edge of the pond he and Ayden had made. It had actually come together quite well and looked no different from those professionally done, surrounded by beautiful flowers. The rays of the sun were glaring down, already causing my bare skin to feel warm.

"Before you start, you said that all I had to do was listen. I've made up my mind and that's final."

"Okay." he replied, pulling off his socks and lying back on his arms.

"I mean it," I spoke again, not believing his unbothered reaction.

"Yes, you've said." He closed his eyes as though he had just come out to sunbathe.

"I'm not joking, I know what's best for me."

"Mmhmm." He nodded, "It's been 108 years...you should by now..."

Growing irritated, I spun on my bottom to face him, still tanning his face.

"Michael!" His eyes shot open and landed on me. "I'm not talking to you as Effy, I'm talking to you as me."

"Okay." He nodded again whilst closing his eyes and leaning back once again, "And once you can tell me who 'me' is, I'll take what you say more seriously."

I took a deep breath, feeling winded by his words and looked at the water looking brighter in the rays of sunlight.

"Look, I'm sorry to be so harsh." Michael sat up and gently touched my shoulder, but I looked away, "I understand you are scared and you've been betrayed before. I also know that you have seen far more than most and been through things we'll never understand, but I think because of all that, you deserve to try and find out who you really are. This might be nothing and these people may be just a bunch of fakes, but it also might be something. It just depends on whether you are brave enough to find out and that's me talking to you, not Effy." He finished before giving my shoulder a squeeze and leaving me on my own.

I sighed deeply, watching the way the water moved with the very gentle breeze in the air. Never had I lived such a life that personally affected me. Even when I did allow myself to get invested, I would usually just be invested as the person I had become, only occasionally would I allow my own feelings come into the picture, but this life had been so much different. I felt like I was losing control over my feelings for the sake of others.

Why are you so frightened? Is it not time to try and find out who you are, instead of stealing the faces of passed souls? What do you have to lose?

As the sun hid behind a cloud, I caught my reflection in the water. Big brown eyes surrounded by a flurry of thick lashes blinked above rosy red cheeks, neither of which belonged to me. They belonged to Effy and always would.

I pulled out my phone from my back pocket.

"Let's do it."

Chapter EIGHT

A niya and her daughter lived in a small fishing village in Devon. It was a perfectly scenic little town with white painted houses and cobblestone streets cascading down to the harbour where boats aligned. We arrived just as the sun was beginning to set its golden glow over the village. Their house wasn't at all what I had imagined, in fact, nothing was how I had imagined. I had expected a house hidden away amongst a forest and surrounded by a garden in disarray but instead, it was one of the white painted houses surrounded by a hundred more with pretty little flower baskets hanging from the windows. I expected Aniya to have dark, perhaps even black, wire-like hair with scary eyes amongst an old, haggard face. She would have a walking stick and an hunched back with fingernails long and dirty. What I discovered instead was that I had watched far too many TV programs and read far too many books. Aniya looked every inch of the stereotype grandmother with white fluffy hair and a kind smile. Her eyes were an almost transparent blue and despite her age, her face was only scattered with a few lines. Though short, she stood tall with no need for an aid and her hands were soft as she took mine into hers. She gave me a suspecting look before smiling.

Aniya welcomed us into her home filled with soft pink furnishings and cream walls and demanded we sat whilst she helped her daughter with beverages. They returned moments later and it was from the look on Ayden's face that I knew Aniya's daughter wouldn't be how he had expected either. She walked in with stunning, blonde locks — you felt yourself wanting to touch them just to see how soft they actually were — and she also had the exact same eyes as her mother. It was hard to believe she was old enough to be Aniya's daughter since she looked so young.

"We're so glad you could all make it." She glided in as though skating on ice with a tray of tea in pretty fine china with Aniya walking slowly behind her.

"I do apologise, but what are your names?" she asked as she placed a cup and saucer in front of each of us before pouring hot tea from a matching teapot.

"I'm Ayden." I quickly shot him a look as he sat in between Michael and I with eyes wide and rosy cheeks.

"And I'm Jennifer and that's John." As I lied, I felt Aniya's eyes on me.

"Well, it's a pleasure for us to meet you. My mother is most intrigued by you, *Mr. Ronaldo*. Perhaps, you could start by telling us about your situation from the beginning?"

"Yes." Ayden looked over at Michael who was trying to hide his laughing mouth with his hand, "Well, you see..." he continued, awkwardly.

I listened as he went on to describe my life and though he pretended it was him - or Mr. Ronaldo, I felt exposed as though everyone could see right through me. I watched Aniya and her daughter listen with curious looks and I felt a prickly heat start in my hands, slowly moving to my arms and face. My breathing became deeper as I struggled to take in any real air and my hearing became distorted as though I was listening from beneath the water.

"Excuse me..." I stood up trying to keep my balance,

"I'm just going pop outside for a moment, please carry on." I said as I headed for the back garden behind us.

I opened the large, sliding doors and breathed in the cool, salty air before walking through the busy garden. It was filled with bushes, flowers and large trees, all overgrown and tall in a way that made it feel like an enchanted garden. Little statues of angels were scattered around amongst the flowers and a worn stone bench sat underneath a weeping willow. I reached out to the hanging branches and let them brush against my skin as I began to cool down before being startled by the noise of someone clearing their throat. I turned to find Aniya walking towards me.

"I thought it was best someone check on you. I know these things can be quite gruelling, especially when having to tell strangers a secret kept for so long." As she finished I watched her carefully as she sat down on the bench.

"I'm fine, just not a fan of travelling."

She nodded, "No, I don't suppose you are, especially after the amount *you* have done."

She spoke so casually, but was it possible that she knew? Had Ayden told her?

"What do you mean?"

Aniya pulled a small bunch of daisies from beside her and began to play with the petals.

"Only that it's a long old drive from London." She smiled, but her answer didn't offer me any relief or confirmation. She looked back down at the daisies in her hand before holding them up, "Don't you think it's peculiar how a daisy is considered a weed and not a flower? It has the look of a flower, it's replicated on clothes and a suitable name for children and pets, but because they thrive in inhospitable environments and are resistant to most pesticides, someone said it's a weed... so it's a weed."

I offered an unsure smile, "Right..."

"Do you want to know another fact about a daisy?" she continued, not waiting for an answer, "They represent innocence and purity and yet, still, they are a weed."

"Interesting... Aniya, perhaps you should go back inside as I'm sure Ay... Mr Ronaldo will want to tell you all about the situation."

"Hmm... Yes, I could go listen to him, but it'll be a lot easier if I just hear it from you."

My heart stopped for a moment as I felt every hair on my body stand, "You know?"

Aniya smiled, "I knew from the moment I set my eyes on you. I could have my sight taken away from me and I would still be able to find a lost soul. Now, come, sit down and tell me your story."

For a moment, I stood still considering running away and forgetting any of this had ever happened, but the little voice in my head whispered repeatedly, *what do we have to lose?*

Taking a deep breath, I sat down and told Aniya everything I could, often forgetting to take a breath as though it was the first time I had ever told anyone. I didn't like to admit it, but talking to Aniya was easy, too easy. She was the first person who didn't look at me with questionable eyes and a doubt in her smile. As cliché as it sounded, it felt like she actually saw me.

"If you would allow me, I'd like to try something on you to see if maybe we can jog your mind for any memories you've suppressed of your true self. Would you allow me to do that?"

I hesitated for a moment, reminding myself I had nothing to lose before nodding as I took her offered hand and went back into the house.

"Ef... I mean, Jennifer, I was just — "

"Ayden, you can stop now. Aniya knows the truth." I said, watching as the panic left his face and was replaced with relief.

"Would you like me to ask them to leave?" Aniya asked whilst signalling for me to lie down on a cream-coloured daybed.

"No, they can stay."

"What are you doing?" Ayden asked the same question etched on Michael's face.

"Helping your friend. Now, silence." Aniya looked at me with a kind smile, "I want you to close your eyes and take some deep breaths and with each one, I want you to hold them in for a count of five, trying only to focus on those breaths."

I did as she instructed, holding each breath whilst counting to five before exhaling.

"I want you to think of each lifetime you have endured in its reverse order, starting with your current. I want you to think of each life as though watching it in rewind, all the way to the first. Try to remember how you felt as each person from the moments before you died to the moment you became them."

As she continued to talk, I became lost watching a rewound film in slow motion. I remembered the happy moments as well as the sad, I felt the pain and suffering of some and the moments of delight in others all the way until John Baldon. I felt the cool tips of Aniya's fingers on either side of my face and though my first reaction was to open my eyes, I couldn't. It was as if I was paralyzed and could only hear her voice as it echoed around me.

"As we reach the beginning of John, I want you to push

past him and look past that darkness as though they are simply murky clouds masking the sun."

I focussed on the darkness, urging for it to leave.

"You're getting closer," Aniya said, but I wasn't. Only darkness surrounded me and the memory of John Baldon. I sighed and tried once more to open my eyes, this time finding myself able to do so, but finding different surroundings.

No longer was I in Aniya's house, but instead on a bridge, looking down at black, lifeless water. I looked around me and noticed that the wooden railings of the bridge were broken with chunks missing. The road was silent with only two dim lights enabling me to see the black tire marks on the road and just like that, a switch had been turned on. I woke up as Effy and sat up in a panic, feeling tears roll down my face.

Aniya squeezed my hands, "Annabella Hart."

"Annabella?" Michael said out loud reminding me that they were still in the room. I wiped my damp face and looked over at their waiting faces, "I remember... I remember who I am."

"How do I look, darling?" my mother said, twirling in her long and narrow purple dress, synched in at the waist with a gold trimming. Though the dress was effortlessly beautiful, much like the girls in Paris, it was the hat she was clearly showing off. It was one the larger hats she owned and had created herself, filled with purple and black feathers and a variety of different lace. My mother had a great eye for fashion and would regularly be found in the room that my father had set aside for her passion and hobby. She had even been approached by designers in the past to work for them, but she always declined, declaring she'd make a bad mother and wife if she worked as well. My mother, unlike myself, did not follow the suffragette movement but instead believed her job would always be taking care of her family, though my father never forced her — he was far too kind to do such a thing. In fact, my father was the type of man who commended the suffragettes and believed that it would be women that would one day rule the world.

"Mama, you look so beautiful, as always!" I smiled as I walked into the house from my part-time job as a shopper's assistant in a store. Whilst none of us needed to work due to the success of my paternal grandfather's oil business, myself and my father both kept a job whilst my older brother was at university, following my father's footsteps in studying medicine.

"Oh, you are too kind, my dear." my mother spoke, flashing her perfect smile and patting her golden curls styled into a coiffure. "Are you sure you wouldn't prefer I stay with you? I'm sure I could persuade your father."

As much as I didn't like to stay at home alone and loved my mother's company, I knew how much my father hated attending his work galas alone, so instead, I shook my head, "No, I will be fine, plus we have Drury Lane to look forward to tomorrow evening."

"Yes, your father was so pleased he got the tickets for you. What a birthday you shall have, Annabella." My mother kissed my forehead as my father walked into the room.

"What's this talk of me, I hear?" he growled in his low voice that would have been enough to strike fear in a person if it wasn't for his kind face. Whilst I loved my mother dearly, it was my father who I idolized. He was the type of man that could hold the room's attention with his witty jokes and bellowing laugh. He seemed to know all that there was to be known and was always being commended for his work as a doctor.

"Nothing but good things, father," I replied as the housekeeper, Catherine, poked at the fireplace causing it to roar in fury at being disturbed.

"I am sure. Now, Rose, we must leave. Annabella, we shall return later this evening with a surprise for you." My mother wrapped her thin arms around me as my father squeezed my shoulder in the way that he did.

"Father, you have spoiled me enough with the theatre tickets!" I beamed watching my parents climbed into the car.

"No such thing for my daughter on her 18th birthday." My father called as they pulled out of the drive and onto the road. I stood waving until the car was out of sight before returning to the house.

"Catherine, perhaps we should have afternoon tea to pass the time?"

"Of course, Miss Annabella, where would you like it?"

"I believe it's your turn to pick, Catherine." I smiled. We had our afternoon tea, played a couple of card games before Catherine excused herself to begin preparations for dinner. Meanwhile, I sat in the living room by the fire reading with the graphophone playing in the background, waiting for my parents to arrive when I heard a car pull into the drive. I listened as the heavy footsteps walked across the path, crunching gravel beneath before climbing the few steps to the door. Catherine left the kitchen and hurried to the door, wiping her hands on her apron before she opened and greeted our guest.

I knew it was not my parents as I hadn't heard more than one set of footsteps, but I wondered if it could have been a surprise, perhaps even my dear brother Albert coming to visit.

"Miss Annabella, I have a guest that would like to see you." Catherine looked uneasy.

"Well, send them in, Catherine," I replied, confused by her hesitation.

The heavy footsteps soon followed Catherine and my heart stopped beating. A figure stood tall and wide in black before me.

He cleared his throat as he removed his hat.

"Miss Hart?"

I nodded, keeping my gaze on his endless black eyes, reminding myself to breathe every few seconds.

"Miss Hart, I'm officer Greg Jenkins. I'm afraid I have some unfortunate news." he said as my stomach began to sink, "Earlier this evening, three people were involved in a car accident on the Emerson Bridge. I'm very sorry to inform you of this, but we believe two of the bodies were your parents."

I froze, feeling my eyes burn as the bile began to creep its way into my throat. As I watched the officer's mouth move underneath a thick and coarse moustache, I wondered if I had become deaf. Everything had become distorted, as though I was submerged under water. A tingling sensation that had started in my fingers had made its way to my chest as a damp prickle crept up my spine. Just as my vision had begun to blur from a mixture of tears and faintness, the officer called my name.

"Did you hear me, Miss Hart?"

I looked up at him, allowing my vision to restore as I wondered how I would break the news to my brother.

"Albert. I need to tell him. Catherine..."

"Miss Hart!" The police officer interrupted me, in a more stern tone.

"Your brother Albert was also involved in the accident. He is in the hospital, but in very serious condition."

As the words left his mouth, so did the strength in my legs.

"He was the surprise," I whispered as the saltiness of my tears reached my mouth.

"Miss Annabella, perhaps we should get you dressed so that you can attend to your brother." I reached for Catherine's hands and forced myself to my feet.

"Officer, I request that you take me to the hospital, please."

He nodded with the faintest look of sympathy.

"Very well, let us go now." I stormed to the door.

"Miss Hart, perhaps you should listen to your housemaid."

"Yes, Miss Annabella, you are not suitably dressed."

I looked at both their concerned faces before looking down at the floor length, white nightgown I was wearing and noticing my long, blonde hair hung around me.

"With all due respect, I've just been informed that my dear parents have passed and my brother is in hospital. Don't you think that I have more pressing matters to consider than ensuring I'm suitably dressed?"

Their faces were expressionless, but the concern still lived in their eyes.

"Officer?"

"Right, yes, Miss Hart." he spoke before walking to the door and leading me to his police car.

I didn't speak another word during the journey but instead, focused on ignoring the sick feeling growing in my stomach. It was almost midnight when we finally arrived, ignoring the looks and whispers that I was attracting as I followed the officer into the hospital. As we approached the nurse's station, I spotted Albert lying peacefully through the glass of the door. I pushed the door open to find him alone in the room with none of the loud noises surrounding the rest of the hospital. Albert laid asleep as I scanned him for any sign of injury, but couldn't find anything except a small graze on the side of his temple. Relief washed over me.

"Dear Albert, you've given me such a fright. When they said your name, my heart broke entirely. I simply could not go on if you had all died, but at least you and I have each other and I'll do all I can to help you recover." I said before taking his hand and noticing the coolness. It was the lump in my throat began to grow did I notice just how still Albert laid.

"No..." I whispered placing my hand on his chest, desperately holding on to the hope of finding it rise or beat.

"Miss Hart," I heard the woman's voice from behind me, but my eyes stayed on Albert's pale face, looking at each sand coloured freckle across his nose and cheeks.

"I'm so sorry." The voice spoke again, "We did all we could, but he had suffered far too much internal damage."

As I listened, the dull ache in my chest grew in strength whilst spreading to cover my entire chest and stomach. It was heavy and wrapped itself around my lungs making each breath I took more difficult than the last. My throat tightened and the burn in my eyes created a wealth of tears. Just as my knees buckled, I let out a cry. Despite already knowing what had happened, it was as though my body didn't and was struggling to digest it.

Not only was I orphaned, but my only sibling had also gone. I was alone with no family left. As a numbness washed over me, I knew what I had to do.

Climbing to my feet, I wiped the dampness from my face with the back of my hand and looked down at Albert. I closed my eyes tight, focusing on the memories I shared with him as I placed a gentle kiss on his cold forehead before walking out of the room and past the officer.

"Miss Hart?" he called, but I let his voice drown amongst the chatter of the nurses and beeps from the many machines. I left the hospital and began the short journey to the bridge where it happened. As my bare feet stepped onto the cold pavement slabs, each step became quicker than the last until the cool air was a wind rushing past me. My lungs expanded, ignoring any tightness felt before as the blinding lights from the cars skimmed over me. I kept going, ignoring the burn in my legs and the ache in my chest. I needed to get there, I needed to see it with my own eyes. I needed to see that it was all real.

The ache in my chest began to consume me and demand that I slow down as my legs started to give up, but it didn't matter as I could see the scene. I stopped a few feet away from the broken gap in the bridge bannister and looked around at the debris sprawled across the road. The street was empty, no cars or people rushing by. It was all so still. As I walked closer to the edge, I imagined the moments where the stillness didn't exist.

My father losing control of the car as he swerved out of the way, the desperate need to protect his family. My mother crying out loud as she looked back at Albert who sat frozen, watching the horror unfold.

I looked down at the black, lifeless water and felt winded as I spotted parts of the car floating on the surface and couldn't help myself from throwing up a mixture of bile and guilt.

"This is all my fault. If you hadn't tried to surprise me..."

I wiped my mouth and pushed my hair away from my face.

"If it is to be your time then it is also to be mine." I said trying to steady my breath as my body became covered with goosebumps.

The loud chime of the bells from Big Ben began to ring as I closed my eyes, seeing the faces of my family. In a few seconds, I would turn 18 years old and it would be a new day, but I wanted neither. I knew whether I jumped or not, my life would never exist past that day.

28 March 1909.

With a deep breath and my thoughts on my family, I allowed myself to fall into nothing but the darkness.

It was darkness that also greeted me as I woke as Effy several hours later. As I sat up from the soft bed beneath me, I tried to remember the day that had just left as the memories of Annabella appeared.

I was Annabella...

Whilst I could remember it all as though it had just

happened, it was strange to know I *was* someone. I had my own identity and not one I had temporarily stolen.

I pushed myself out of the blankets as I tried to work out my surroundings. In the darkness, I could make out the silhouettes of the furniture in the room, an empty dressing table, a sparingly filled bookcase and a perfectly made bed sitting opposite to the messy one I had just been lying in. Pictures hung on the walls, but I couldn't make them out. I wondered if we were in Aniya's house as I tried to remember what happened after I discovered the truth. Everything seemed so foggy.

I twisted the door handle carefully and walked out into the hallway. It was just as dark but with several closed doors displaying little plaques. I walked past them, reading the different numbers on each. As I reached the end of the hallway, I found a staircase leading to another hallway and also glass patio doors that were slightly open. I slipped through the gap and into the garden, overlooking the silent sea, lit only by the light of the moon. I followed the stone path, through the bushes and trees, until I reached a short wooden gate. From where I stood, I could make out the dark silhouette of someone sat on the beach facing the glistening black water. Curious, I slid my feet out of my socks and stepped out of the garden onto the cool, damp sand, it crumbled in between my toes as I walked towards to silhouette. As I grew closer, I watched as the person idly played with the sand before catching the side of their face, lit only by the moon.

"A little bit creepy, don't you think?" Ayden spoke without turning to face me.

"What?" I replied feeling as though I had been caught spying. I sat beside him, brushing the sand off my hands waiting for his reply.

"How, on the surface, the sea looks lifeless but underneath lives millions of animals..."

"Yes, I suppose that is... creepy." I looked at him with a confused glance.

"No, I mean..." he paused and looked at me. The light of the moon still pouring down on his face.

"I mean, it's weird how something can look like one thing, but be so much more."

"Oh." I looked down at my feet in the sand, feeling each grain between each toe, "you mean, like me?"

I felt his eyes on me, but kept my own straight ahead before he sighed loudly.

"You know, I didn't *not* believe you, but I also don't think I actually believed it was possible."

I let his words wash out with the shore, not knowing what to do with them.

"Do you remember it all?"

I nodded, "Yes, I remember." I said clearing my throat. "What did Aniya tell you? I don't remember much of what happened."

"Well, you started fitting and shouting names and words, but she kept saying it was normal and then you just stopped and went limp. It was like you were dead, but Aniya said you wouldn't wake for a while after so your dad... I mean, Michael, took you to bed and then Aniya told us what she saw."

"And what did she see?"

"Your life as Annabella up until you jumped. Hey..." his sudden cold hand on my bare arm caused me to jump, "I'm sorry to hear about your family."

I smiled weakly and nodded my head, unsure of how I actually felt. On one hand, it felt like it had happened yesterday — as if the final piece of my puzzle had been found — but on the other hand, I didn't feel like I was Annabella. I felt great sadness, but I couldn't tell if it was because I had heard a sad and unfortunate story or if it was because the story belonged to me.

Even though I had been doing it for over a hundred years, like Ayden, I was questioning how this had happened. This was the real world, people didn't just die and wake up in other people's bodies, stuck as a 17-year-old. I needed to speak with Aniya. I had a thousand questions causing a whirlwind in my mind and I knew she would be the only person who could even attempt to answer them.

"What are you thinking?"

I looked up at Ayden's face, taking a moment, allowing myself to become distracted by the concern he displayed.

"I... I honestly have no idea. I have spent so many years trying to find out what was wrong with me and why this was happening, but I always felt like the real me existed somewhere, I just..." I paused, "I've spent over a hundred years being someone else, I don't know if I know how to be... me."

"Hey, you've only just found out who you are, and that brings all of its own memories and pain." Ayden leant to his side and gently knocked into me, "You discovered something today that you never thought you would. It's okay to not understand it all right now. Give yourself some time."

I nodded, wondering if time would really change anything.

"What about you? How do you feel about all of this? You don't have to stick around if this is all too much."

Ayden placed his hand on top of my own, resting on my bent knee and gently squeezed, "I don't care if you are Effy, Annabella or my crazy neighbour Jim, I'm not going anywhere. I'm here with you all the way."

I matched his soft smile and leant into his body, resting my head on his shoulder. Beyond the sounds of the waves hitting the shore smoothly, I listened to a deep and continuous thud coming from underneath his loose shirt.

"How cold do you think that water is?" he asked whilst his chest vibrated underneath me.

"Cold."

"Well, that will make this interesting then," Ayden said, pulling his trainers off and pushing himself off the ground.

"What are you doing?" I watched carefully as he pulled off his shirt to reveal the body he had gained from years of playing football and working out. I held my breath for a moment as he reached for the button on his jeans.

"I've never swum at night before." he replied, shuffling out of his jeans so that they slowly dropped past his black briefs and tanned legs until they reached his ankles.

"So, you're going to try now?"

A smirk began to grow at the corners of his mouth as he stepped out of the trousers and nodded, "Seems too good of an opportunity to pass up."

I chuckled as he began to walk towards the black sea water in nothing but his briefs and white socks.

"Are you coming?" He looked back as he reached the soft waves hitting the sand.

I shook my head vigorously, "Not a chance."

"Oh, don't be such a party pooper. What's the worst that can happen?"

"You mean aside from drowning or getting attacked by a shark? I much prefer to swim when I can see what is around me, thanks."

Ayden began to laugh whilst shaking his head, "I'd like to start by reminding you that this is Devon, I highly doubt there are any sharks lurking around and secondly, even if there were, you're immortal..."

"I may not be able to die, but I can still catch the flu." I screwed up my face feeling nervous as Ayden began to walk towards me, still continuing to laugh.

"Oh, the flu... any more excuses?"

"They are not excuses." I rolled my eyes as though dismissing his comment, but actually it was so that I would stop looking at his chest. There was no doubt about it, Ayden was very easy on the eyes, especially when he was in the mood and basking in the moonlight.

He stopped laughing, but kept the smirk across his lips, "Fine, have it your way. Would you pass my trousers, please?"

As I picked up the jeans and offered them to him, his hand wrapped around my arm and pulled me up onto my feet. Seconds later, I was bent over Ayden's shoulder.

"Ayden, put me down!" I shouted, lightly hitting his back as my hair dangled under me.

"Nope." he said beginning to jog towards the water.

"But, my clothes are going to get drenched, Ayden!"

"Your own fault." He said whilst laughing and as he ran into the water, I felt the splashes of water hit my arms and face before being completely submerged into the coldness.

"Oh, you little git," I said trying to sound irritated but I couldn't help but smile once I had resurfaced with my hair stuck to every part of my face and the bitter taste of the sea in my mouth.

"You look like something out of a horror movie." Ayden laughed, pointing out the mascara that was now running down my face in streaks.

I screwed up my face, shooting him a look before using my hands to continuously splash him. He continued to laugh before diving into the water and grabbing my legs to pull me under again. Losing all balance I grabbed onto him, wrapping my arms around his neck until we resurfaced again, but this time, I was a couple of inches taller than him. I looked down at his damp face, watching the little drops of water let go of his hair and begin a slow descend down his face. For a second, I wished my fingers were doing the same.

Moving my gaze to his eyes, I held my breath for a moment, finding he was looking right back at me. His beautiful green eyes and yet just simply saying they were green was just like saying the grass was green. It was sufficient, but didn't nearly capture the entire beauty of them. Like a mosaic, there were splashes of green around a ring of auburn flames that circled his pupil.

My arms felt as though they were beginning to give way, slowly slipping from his neck to his broad shoulders as my body continued to slide down his until my toes touched the ground. I waited for Ayden to release his arms from my waist, both of us aware I no longer needed the support, but his grip remained as steady as his gaze.

During our unlikely friendship, I had come to discover the many sides of Ayden. I had seen him as an angry and cocky kid whilst at school, a vulnerable and sensitive boy when talking about his mum and I had seen him as the caring and protective person he was when being my friend, but I had never seen this Ayden.

I had always been aware of Ayden's good looks. His dark hair and olive skin highlighting his green eyes just like the sky and sand highlighted the beauty of the sea. Just a flash of his torso would strike most with a moment of silence as you followed the dark shadows around each muscle.

But it was the way he looked at you, keeping you close to him, but still a few inches away so that he left you questioning the moment and what his next move would be. And you could tell he enjoyed causing the questions as the corners of his mouth curled mischievously.

As I watched his face, I imagined what would happen next. He'd lean in for a kiss and I wouldn't stop him. It wouldn't be long before I kissed him back and we'd wake up the next morning questioning whether our friendship could lead to something more. Feelings would soon grow stronger and before we'd know it, we'd be inseparable and fall hopelessly in love, but the looming date would soon arrive — just like it always did — and I would leave him to live another life knowing that one day, all I would be to him was a memory.

I had done it before and no matter how many years and lives I had lived, I was still just a 17-year-old girl that didn't want to be left alone again whilst watching life go on without me.

So despite being more than aware of the fact that I liked Ayden more than a friend and wanting so badly to give in to the protests of my body, I closed my eyes and allowed my mouth to end the moment.

"Ayden, I don't think this a good idea..."

As I spoke, I watched the corners of his mouth uncurl and stiffen, just as his body did, as if he was nothing more than a plank of wood.

Quickly, his face changed from a blank gaze to a laugh, so over the top, as though I had said the funniest thing in the world.

"I can't believe you thought I was being serious!" He shook his head in laughter and perhaps if it hadn't been for the red in his cheeks and the faintest look of hurt in his eyes, I would have believed him, "I was just trying to distract you... you know, after today... don't worry... " He continued to laugh as he took several steps away from me, "We're just friends, I don't see you in that way…"

I smiled weakly and slowly nodded my head as I began to walk back to the shore, "Great, well, I best get back to the room and dry off." I replied.

Even though I knew that if I hadn't spoken he would have kissed me, I still felt bruised by his words.

I don't see you in that way…

Once back into the house, I carefully climbed the stairs and as my eyes adjusted to the darkness, I noticed several pictures of Aniya, her daughter and who I imagined to be the rest of her family. They all had the same light hair and the big almond shaped eyes that Aniya's daughter had. As I approached the door to the room I had woken in, I found a drawing of a young Aniya. Even as a drawing she looked beautiful with curly blonde locks and cheekbones that rivalled a catwalk model but what drew you in was her smile. The same knowing smile she had displayed earlier. A smile that made you feel both safe and exposed. Thankful for the moments distraction, I walked into the bedroom and quickly showered off the wet sand that had managed to get everywhere. With nothing but the sound of my own breathing and shaken heartbeat, I began to replay the awkward moment over again. I wished I had just let it happen and, for once, revelled in the unknown, but instead I was alone, lying on a bed doubting whether Ayden had liked me at all.

I don't see you in that way…

After about thirty minutes of tossing and turning, unable to get out of the ever-closing room filled with my worries and concerns, I heard the faintest footsteps walking up the stairs and across the landing. Quickly, I rolled over so that my back faced the door and held my eyes shut.

When the door opened, I felt a surge of butterflies flutter in my stomach as I tried to remember how a sleeping person might breathe, because I was pretty sure what I was doing looked as though I was having some type of an attack.

I didn't want to speak to him. I had already convinced myself that I had read it all wrong and he did, in fact, not see me in that way. Of course that should have been a good thing because it meant I had nothing to worry about but instead, I felt stupid.

I had done this enough times to know better.

The door closed gently and the footsteps paused for a moment.

Breathe, Effy, Annabella, whoever you bloody are, just breathe...

The problem was, I could no longer control my breathing. It was either erratic or non existent.

The footsteps began again, this time what sounded like around the bed. I knew it was Ayden and that he was standing close by from his smell mixed with the salt of the sea water.

It went silent again, no sign of footsteps or any type of movement and just as the silence was beginning to give me a headache, Ayden whispered.

"Are you awake?"

With all my strength, I tried to keep my eyelids from flickering and my breathing from looking abnormal, but there was no chance of controlling my heartbeat. I could hear it thumping away so loud in my ears that I wondered if he could hear it too.

After a few painfully long seconds, Ayden sighed and walked towards the bathroom, closing the door behind him. Moments later, I heard the shower begin to run and I exhaled as though I had spent the last five minutes holding my breath.

I wondered for a moment what he would have said had I opened my eyes. Surely it wouldn't have been to reiterate what he had said earlier. Could he have wanted to take it all back?

What does it matter? You stopped it from happening, remember?

I sighed quietly and curled up into a ball, urging for sleep to arrive before Ayden returned, but it didn't. Quickly, I shut my eyes once again and pulled the covers to my face, pretending I was fast asleep as Ayden opened the door and walked back into the room. Ignoring the beating coming from in my chest, I listened as Ayden walked around the room until everything became silent.

With my curiosity getting the better of me, I slowly raised the blankets even higher to cover most of my face and peeked out to find Ayden looking at his phone. A light coming from outside, shone through the windows directly onto him revealing his naked torso and the towel wrapped around his waist. He looked deep in thought as he stared down at the phone, only tapping on the screen when the light dimmed. I watched him as he sat on the edge of the bed, slouching over his phone, causing the muscles in his shoulders to tense. I felt a rush of excitement in my stomach again, wanting to just keep watching the last few drops of water roll down his back.

I closed my eyes and allowed myself a moment to wonder what it would be like to trace the paths the water drops had taken but with my own fingers. The wanting feelings I had for Ayden weren't dissimilar to those I had with Walter Valentine, in fact, that night, it felt like it could have even been stronger. The problem was, I couldn't tell if it was because I had told myself I couldn't have him or the possibility that he didn't want me.

What's really holding you back, Annabella?

I had no real answer, at least none that seemed valid in that moment. I wanted him and there was a chance he wanted me. So what that I might get my heart broken when the 28th March came around. Wouldn't I regret the missed opportunity more? The date was coming whether I liked it or not, didn't I deserve a few lifetimes of happiness?

Opening my eyes, ready to jump out of the bed, I noticed Ayden walking towards the bedroom door, with his phone still in his hand. Unable to move, I watched him open the door and leave the room.

Was Ayden with someone else? Was it Brogan?

Hearing the muffle of his voice from behind the door, I climbed out of the bed, needing to hear who he was talking to.

With my ear pressed against the door, I listened as he whispered.

"...I don't know what to do... I know I said the wrong thing."

I wondered if it was me he was talking about as I tried to listen for more, but he had walked further away so all I could hear was just the hum of his low voice.

What was wrong with me? This was unlike me. I seemed to have lost all control of myself. All I could think about was Ayden. As my hand hovered over the door handle, I urged myself to open it, but instead my hand remained still, just as the rest of me did until the door was opened. Panicked, I followed the door and remained still in the darkness as Ayden walked into the room, still in his towel, looking at my empty bed. I watched his glance move to the bathroom door, which was opened with the light switched off.

"Annabella?" he called in a voice slightly louder than a whisper. I realised it was the first time he had called me by my real name.

I didn't say anything in return, but instead slowly stepped out of the darkness causing him to spin on his heel from the noise of my footsteps.

"What are you doing over there?"

I ignored his question and instead took a deep breathe, feeling the bile rise to my throat.

"Are you okay?" he asked again and this time, I shook my head.

"Ayden, tell me, why would this be a bad idea?" I whispered, watching his face quickly figure out what I meant.

"I didn't say it was."

My heart skipped a beat as I tried to steady my nerves. His face remained serious.

"Then tell me again, why don't you see me in that way?"

His eyes dropped to the floor, but he didn't say a word.

Feeling my heart fall from my chest into the pits of my stomach, I turned to face the door and leave the room when I felt a hand grab hold of my arm.

"Annabella..." Ayden spoke and the way he said my name robbed me of breath.

I faced him, watching his eyes flicker across my face as he pulled me towards him so that our hips brushed.

"What?"

His eyes didn't leave me as he quickly cupped my jaw and pulled my face to him so that I was a mere few centimetres from his lips.

"I lied." he said with eyes that grabbed onto my soul and as the words left his mouth, his lips were on mine.

At first, the kiss was hesitant as though we were both doing it for the first time or perhaps we were both scared the other would pull away, but we didn't. Instead, using his shoulders as an aid, I grew on my tiptoes, pulling him into me.

It wasn't long before the kiss changed and no longer were there signs of hesitation but only an urgency to feel closer to each other. Suddenly, Ayden pulled away, still cradling my face, scanning my eyes for a moment of doubt. I stared back, impatiently waiting for his lips to be back on my own.

"I'm sorry about what I said earlier..." Ayden tried to talk, but I stopped him by moving my hand to his mouth.

"Just kiss me." I pleaded, longingly.

I uncovered his mouth to reveal a smirk that filled my lungs with air and stomach with excitement.

"No..." he whispered, smirk and all, "you kiss me."

I bit my bottom lip, relishing the mischievous look in Ayden's eyes before carefully placing each hand on the side of his face. I stepped closer to him so that our noses touched and our lips brushed as I placed a kiss on the corner of his smiling mouth. That was all Ayden needed before he scooped my legs up from beneath me and wrapped them around his waist. Soon after, his hands ran across my back, travelling under my T-shirt. His touch sent shivers up my spine. I was so lost in the kiss that I had hardly noticed that Ayden had walked across the room to my bed. With ease, he threw me onto the bed before crawling over me, dipping low so that I felt his breath against the part of my stomach that was no longer covered. Slowly, Ayden grabbed each side of my T-shirt, gently pushing it up as he placed kisses across my stomach, working upwards. I daren't breathe in fear I would explode. Every part of my body felt alive.

As he approached the edges of my bra, he paused and looked up at me.

Answering the question on his face, I sat up and pulled off my top before wrapping my arms around his neck and pulling his face to mine. I was becoming to realise that no matter how intense or passionate the kiss, I would never have enough of it. I wanted to be closer to him. I had kissed my fair share of boys over the years, but I knew at that moment none matched this. Not even Walter.

I relished the feeling of his weight on top of me, feeling every part of his naked torso on my bare skin. I stopped breathing as I felt his hands confidently make their way to the edges of my jeans, gently tugging at the hoops before moving to the button. Inside, I was screaming and jumping around — like you would when watching the moment the boy kisses the girl in a film — except this wasn't a film and I was the girl that the boy was kissing.

"Are you sure you want to do this?" Ayden said breathlessly, positioned to unbutton my jeans.

I bit my lip once again, this time harder in an attempt to stop myself from screaming. Instead, I smiled and whispered, "I've never been surer of something in any life." And just like that, Ayden and I would no longer ever be 'just' friends.

Chapter NINE

"A nnabella?" I heard, whispered in the most delicate way as I woke from what felt like a decade of sleep.

"Annabella, are you okay?" The voice spoke again before I realised the name belonged to me. I wearily opened my eyes and sat up to find Aniya's daughter smiling back at me.

"I'm fine, what time is it?" I asked as I rubbed my eyes, noticing I had been alone in the room with Ayden's bed still neatly made as it was the night before.

"It's just after midday. My mother thought that maybe if you felt rested enough that it was time to have a chat with you."

I nodded, "Where is everyone?"

What I really meant was where was Ayden and why was he not the one waking me up.

"Mr. Garcia and Ayden are downstairs. Why don't you get yourself ready and come down too? I can imagine you must have a lot of questions." I felt a twinge of sadness as she referred to Michael as Mr. Garcia and no longer as my dad. She smiled again and I knew she was just trying to be nice, but I felt irritated by her, as if she could really know what was going through my mind.

"Thanks for waking me," I replied as politely as I could as I climbed out of the bed and walked into the bathroom.

I didn't know what to focus on most, the night before and the lack of Ayden when I woke up or my impending conversation with Aniya. It was obvious that she knew what she was doing, but in truth I wasn't sure if I trusted her or if I thought she could do anything further to help me or Effy.

As Effy's face greeted me in the mirror, I tried to remember my own. Unlike Effy, my features were fair. Instead of Effy's brown and naturally straight hair, I had long and slightly wavy hair, as though I had gone to sleep with plaits in, that was almost the shade of white. My eyes were the cool shade of blue and my skin made Effy's fair skin seem bronzed. As I looked ahead, I wondered if I had shut my eyes and started dreaming. Looking back at me in the mirror was no longer Effy but Annabella. I reached up to my face, touching my skin, brushing over my soft and flushed cheeks, noticing the many Auburn freckles scattered over my nose and spotting a small, pink scar on my chin. The memories of a not-so-recent horse riding accident resurfaced.

"Annabella?" The knock on the door startled me as Aniya's daughter called out.

"Yes?"

"I have placed some clean clothes on the bed for you. I think we're the same size, but do let me know if none of the options are suitable."

Feeling a twinge of guilt for my earlier tone with her, I opened the door and found her cheery face.

"Thank you, I appreciate it." I smiled.

"You're most welcome, Annabella." She returned the smile and left the room.

Returning to the bathroom, I looked back into the mirror and was disappointed to find Effy was back.

Even though I didn't feel connected to the former name and face that belonged to me, it was the most familiar thing I had come across yet. Like an old friend I hadn't seen in many years.

I splashed some water on my face and allowed the cool breeze from the opened window in the bedroom to dry it off as I began to investigate the pile of clothes that had been left.

Aniya's daughter had been right, we did share the same clothes size, however, it was evident we didn't share the same style. Throwing anything floral or polka dot to one side, I was left with a pair of light denim skinny jeans and a loose white Bardot top. I put on Effy's converses before tying my hair up into a messy bun and leaving the room, taking a deep breath as I found the last step. I felt my hands begin to sweat as I picked the skin around my nails.

"Annabella!" Aniya said excitedly. I enjoyed listening to her say my name, making it sound much more exotic than it was.

"Hello," I said, feeling awkward as I felt the room staring at me. The thought of looking at Ayden in the eyes made my stomach flip, so I kept my eyes on the ground as I found an empty spot beside Aniya.

"Perhaps we should speak alone?" Aniya asked, sensing my uneasiness. Before I could agree with her, I caught the look of concern on Michael's face. I knew he was worried about me, but I also knew he was more concerned about what this all meant for his daughter's body. I wondered for a second if he thought there was a chance that Effy could return.

"It's fine, let them stay," I said looking up and catching Ayden's careful smile.

"Very well." Aniya nodded and took my hand into hers as I flinched at her touch.

She gently patted my hand and looked at me like a grandmother might comfort her grandchild. A gentle reassurance to remind you that you were safe.

"I'd like to first say that I'm very sorry for your loss, Annabella. I can imagine it was very difficult to have to remember that all over again, especially since you probably don't feel very connected to your original life."

"Why is that?" I interrupted, "I mean, I know it was me and I remember everything, the memories, the feelings and everything else, but I don't feel like it's..."

"You?" Aniya finished for me and I nodded. As much as I was thankful to have Michael and Ayden believe me and want to help me, it was a relief to have someone that understood. It was like Aniya had really seen it all before.

"It's been 109 years since you were last Annabella, that is 109 people you've had to become, discovering new things with each life. Some might have liked cheese, others might have hated it and as you went on, working around your new discoveries, parts of you got lost."

I tried to think back to my first life as someone else and tried to find the similarities I had with the real me.

"But wait, I didn't know anything about Annabella...I mean, me. I woke up as John with no memory of anything."

Aniya nodded as though she had expected my reply.

"Annabella, I follow a spiritual belief that believes in many things and one of those things is that every soul or spirit can sometimes leave its body. We call this soul travelling. Normally, this is done temporarily, usually when a person sleeps or takes a type of drug. More often than not, the cause is stress as people are distracted and have a feeling of losing control but other times, it's forced, like using drugs."

All three of us nodded in sync.

"I, myself, have never come across a case like yours, Annabella, but I have heard many stories of lost souls and yesterday, after speaking with you, I spoke with my mentors and those that have helped souls similar to yours." Aniya paused for a moment, squeezing my hand slightly and shifting her bottom so that she faced me.

"The moment you decided you were going to jump off that bridge, you were already suffering from a great deal of stress and in a state of absolute grief. As you jumped, your body went into shock and so, to escape the trauma, your soul jumped. The problem was, when your soul went to go back into your body, it was too late and it had already died."

Despite having already guessed that I had died as Annabella, I felt almost winded as Aniya confirmed it. I had committed suicide. Just as Effy had.

"So why didn't my soul just die with my body?" I asked.

"Because your soul wasn't in the body at the time of passing. Your body was dead, but your soul was very much alive. A living soul cannot pass into the other realm so it found another body."

"But, how does it take another body when the person has died?" Ayden spoke reminding me that Aniya and I were not alone.

"It may sound confusing, but when a death occurs, your soul passes first and then your body. Even if it's only for a few seconds, your body is alive but with no soul and Annabella's soul linked to the first one available."

"Aniya, if that's the case then why do I never live for more than 364 days a year? Why do I always die on 28th March?" I asked.

She smiled weakly, "Because you were never supposed to live past that date."

A wave of sadness washed over me as I realised this was confirmation that I was stuck doing this forever. I would die over and over again, only now I knew why.

"So what does this mean? Is there no way to stop it from happening?" Michael asked, but I was certain I knew the answer until Aniya opened her mouth.

"Yes, there is." All eyes shot over to her, including my own. Surely it was not possible for me to stay as Effy?

"The only way to stop this from happening, Annabella, is to put you back in your original body."

"How is that possible? Her body is dead." Ayden's face spoke all scrunched up.

"Yes," Aniya answered and immediately I knew what she had meant.

"You can put me back in my body, but I would have to die, for real this time..."

"Yes." She nodded and I copied, staring at a half empty glass of water on the table.

My stomach was greeted with a mixture of bile and butterflies. I had spent the majority of my soul jumping years wishing there was an end, praying with all my might to any god or universe that listened to just let it all end and just as I had given up and accepted that it was always going to be this way, I was given a possibility. This was what I had wanted for so long and yet, looking at Michael and Ayden, I was unsure.

"She is not going to just die. Can you not just do something to keep her in Effy's body?" Ayden was on his feet, talking in a much less polite voice than we had seen before.

"As much as I would love to say I could, it simply isn't possible, Ayden. Annabella has two choices, she either continues as she is and will leave this body just as she has done with the others or she returns back to her body and she passes away as she was meant to."

"This is ridiculous, obviously she isn't going to just give up, right, Annabella?" Ayden looked at me with red cheeks, pinched brows and look of panic that caused my heart to ache. He had suffered so much loss already, his dad and older siblings who had left him alone with a mum that had given up so many times. How could he understand that it might be my time when all he knew me as was a 17-year-old girl and not the 17-year-old girl who had lived 109 times.

I closed my eyes and looked down at the floor, "Right."

With Ayden in a furious mood with Aniya and Michael not knowing what to do, we decided it was time we made our way home. As we said our goodbyes to Aniya and her daughter, Aniya pulled my arm back and held onto to me, "Annabella, just remember, a choice doesn't have to be made today, you have until 28th March. I am here." With a stomach wrecked with nerves, I thanked her before walking off to the car, unsure if I would ever see her again.

Once in the car, I pulled my headphones out of my bag as I could already tell that Ayden was going to try and talk about it all.

"I can't believe that woman..."

"Ayden!" I said a little sterner than I had expected, "I don't want to talk about it right now." I watched his face sink before looking at Michael beside him and then out of the window.

I wasn't interested in anything either of them said, not at that moment anyway. My head was drowning in a hundred and one worries and none seemed to be about me. Wanting to escape it all and not being able to leave a driving car, I settled for sleep and spread myself across the empty back seat. I was met with a dream shortly after closing my eyes, but not one of preference.

Without even having to look, I knew I was in my own body. As I opened my eyes, I took a sharp, short breathe recognising the broken bridge I was stood on the edge of. I watched as bits of debris floated with the current, disappearing underneath the bridge when I was suddenly hit with an overwhelming feeling that I should jump. I knew I didn't want to jump, but every part of my body was ready and willing to, as though I had no say.

Resisting as much as I could, I felt my body beginning to lean forward, almost in slow motion. I felt the gravity beneath me pull me down as my feet left the bridge and I began to slowly fall. To anyone else watching, it would have seemed as if I was simply floating to the surface but I soon found myself submerged into the black water. As I began to sink under, I noticed I wasn't breathing, as though I didn't need to. I couldn't feel the temperature of the water, but I could feel it glide against my skin and through the gaps of my fingers and toes. Even in the darkness, I could tell the water was lifeless or so I thought.

Still being gently pulled down, I noticed the water beginning to lighten, not so much that I could see clearly, but enough so that I could make out the things around me. It was as I looked down that I noticed I was approaching the river bed and a black 1908 Ford in perfect condition beneath me. Immediately, I recognised it as my parent's car and the sound of my heartbeat echoed loudly around me. As my feet touched the rough floor made up of rocks and debris, I noticed I was no longer being pulled around, but had full control of where I went and yet I still didn't begin to float as I should have. Hesitant, but full of curiosity, I walked towards the car, relieved to find it was empty and the black interior still intact. Confused, I continued to walk around the car until I reached the back and began to hear a faint noise of banging and screams of help coming from inside. Terror rooted me to the spot as I noticed it grow in volume until it was all I could hear. Feeling the force behind me once again, I began to walk around the car with a rising burning sensation of bile in my throat. I closed my eyes tight, terrified of where the muffled screams led to until I could feel the smoothness of the cool windows and all went very quiet. Cautiously, I opened my eyes to find the car empty. My chest was vibrating with the rapid beating of my heart as my stomach continued to knot itself tight. Slowly, I leaned forward when suddenly I stumbled backwards and onto the hard floor at the sight of my mother and father, desperately banging against the windows. Even though I was fully aware it was all a dream, I couldn't help myself but feel a rush of panic as I stumbled to my feet and raced over to the car.

"Mother," I yelled as I pulled at the handle unable to open it. Quickly, I tried the other door where the face of my father began to grow an icy shade of blue.

"Father." I cried, feeling my eyes begin to sting as I continued desperately trying to open the door. My chest ached as the familiar feeling of pain hit me. The feeling of losing my family all over again. This was my dream, why couldn't I save them?

I began to sob as I watched their muffled plea's stop,

their hands fall and their lives slip away. Allowing myself to fall, I closed my eyes unable to watch anymore and begging for the dream to come to an end when I began to hear people shouting and the sound of metal wheels against the floor. I opened my eyes to find myself at the same hospital I had seen many years before. A stretcher was being wheeled in by doctors that shouted orders at nurses whilst they raced into the room behind them. I knew it was my brother even though I couldn't see his face. The doors closed in front of me, leaving me with only a small window to watch the events unfold. Doctors ripped his shirt open as the nurses cleared the area before the doctors began resuscitation. I just watched on as the heavy pounds to his chest caused his arm to fall lifelessly beside him until the doctors stopped and looked at each other with a look of disappointment before they looked at their pocket watches and left the room.

I could see Albert's face clearly now. His wet hair stuck to his face with nothing more than a blank expression. No sign of anything but peace. My chest continued to ache as I felt a warm tear fall down my face. Moments after the nurses had finished cleaning him up, I arrived wearing the same white dress that I was currently stood in with the police officer beside me. The sound of my bare feet hitting the stone floor went in time of my beating heart as I watched the former me buckle to the floor and let out a cry that you could feel tear you apart.

"Annabella?" I could hear faintly as I followed the former me out of the hospital and eventually onto the bridge.

"Annabella..."

Despite the tears on my face, I looked calm in those

final moments as the realisation of what I was going to do surfaced.

"Annabella..."

As the clock loudly chimed in the background, I took no deep breaths or looked back but simply took one step forward and fell into the darkness.

"Annabella..."

I closed my eyes and once I opened them, I found Michael and Ayden peering over at me.

"Are you okay?" Michael asked as I grew familiar to my surroundings of the car.

"We're back now. I think you were having a bad dream." Ayden spoke.

I nodded, wishing it had only just been a dream.

Climbing out of the car, I looked at Effy's house with a slight feeling of dread growing in the pit of my stomach. I would have to pretend to be Effy again. I'd have live her life, use her things whilst pretending her family were my own when really, mine were gone and the real me existed. At least, she did in my memory.

"Come on, you've had a stressful couple of days, I think you deserve to relax in bed for the rest of the day," Michael said, stretching an arm around me.

"Annabella?" Ayden's cool fingers wrapped around my arm just like it had the previous night except I wasn't greeted with the same feeling.

"Look, I know this has been crazy for you, but I'm glad

you have chosen to carry on. I think you've made the right decision."

I took a deep breath as Michael excused himself.

"Ayden, you have absolutely no idea what I am going through..." I said, feeling myself begin to choke up and my eyes becoming blurry, "because if you did, you would never have assumed I would want to continue."

"Annabella..." Ayden tried to speak.

"No. Just no. You'll never understand what it feels to lose your entire family and feel so devastatingly alone that you're only solution is to end it all. And *then* for 108 years, you are tortured by having to live and die another life, suffering in ways you wouldn't even be able to imagine, with no sign of an ending. You'll never understand how tired I am, Ayden, how much I just want this to end." I stopped and wiped my wet face with the back of my hand.

"You're right, I have no idea what any of that is like, but I do know that I care about you, Annabella and I'm not ready to just let you leave my life." he shouted at me with anger in his voice, but sadness in his eyes. "So, if last night meant anything to you then I ask you... no, I beg you, please give me some time to prove to you why you should stay... please?"

I watched his eyes flicker across my face waiting for my answer.

"I need to be alone right now, Ayden. I need time to think, okay?"

He nodded slowly before turning his back to me and walking away.

"Ayden?" I called.

"What?"

I took a breath, "I care about you, too."

He nodded again, "Okay."

"Come on, love, let's get you inside," Michael said, appearing beside me and placing his arm around my shoulders, guiding me up to Effy's bedroom.

"Do you want to talk?" he asked as he sat beside me on the bed.

I sighed out loud and allowed myself to fall back onto the soft covers behind me.

"I don't know. It's just so much to take in." I rubbed my face and closed my eyes, still amazed at the tiredness I felt after the amount of sleep I had had in the past two days.

"It is. It must be very confusing for you."

I sat up and faced Michael, "That's the thing, it's not confusing at all. I have lived for so long thinking I was being punished for something with no possibility of it ending. I have spent the last 108 years being someone else, watching the world change and the people in it leave for good, wishing I could just do the same. Today, I find out that my wish could become a reality and it's like a terminally ill patient finding out that their suffering could come to an end with a possible cure."

Michael nodded gently and pulled me into his chest.

"I care about Ayden, but he doesn't understand that I don't get to just stay as Effy. This life will end just like the others did and I will become someone else again. I don't want to do it again."

"I know, and you don't have to do anything you don't want to do. Look, I heard what Aniya said, you don't have to decide right now. You have until the 28th of March to figure it all out so why don't you enjoy the time that's left and see how you feel closer to the time." Michael weakly smiled, "If you still want to go ahead with it then we will get in contact with Aniya and you can speak with Ayden. If you don't want to do it, then we'll figure that out too."

I nodded and didn't say another word that day as I gradually fell asleep despite the thoughts that spun around in my head.

My mind wouldn't change.

Come 28th March, Effy Garcia would be the last.

Chapter TEN

A chilly breeze brushed against my bare skin as I slowly woke up from a deep sleep filled with many dreams that I couldn't remember once I had opened my eyes. Rolling over to my side, I felt the coolness from my phone screen against my arm and once lit, I could see a text message from Ayden saying goodnight. His pleading face resurfaced in my mind, filling me with the same guilt I had felt the day before. Shaking it off, I dropped the phone beside me before pulling out Effy's laptop. The bright light glared back at me, waiting for me to type.

Annabella Hart.

At first, the results displayed several social media accounts with pictures of girls pouting or with dog ears, but as I clicked onto the second page, I found what I was looking for.

FATAL MOTOR CAR ACCIDENT

An inquest was held yesterday at Ballymore Hall, London, on the bodies of Mr. M Hart, his wife, Mrs. R Hart and their son, Albert Hart who all succumbed to injuries sustained in a motor car accident on Emerson Bridge, London. The deceased were taking a ride in a motor car owned by Mr. M Hart when the brakes refused to act and the motor car crashed into the bridge and went into the river. A verdict of 'accidental death' was reached. Meanwhile, the case of their missing daughter has occupied the attention of the local police. Annabella Hart mysteriously disappeared ten days ago on the night of her family's fatal motor car accident and although an anxious search has been continuously made since her disappearance, no trace of her can be found.

"They never found my body?" I whispered out loud, imagining my body after 109 years in the river. Shrugging off the disturbing thoughts, I closed the laptop and went back to the phone.

Effy Garcia: Ayden, I'm sorry about yesterday.

I didn't have to wait long for a response as the three little dots appeared to tell me Ayden was typing.

Ayden West: It's okay. It's me who should actually be apologizing.

I smiled as I sat up and leant back on the headboard.

Effy Garcia: Look, even though my decision is unlikely to change, I do want to spend the rest of my time with you, Ayden.

As the three little dots appeared as quickly as they disappeared, I wondered what he was actually thinking.

Ayden West: Would you say it was impossible for me to change your mind?

Effy Garcia: Nothing is impossible, but highly unlikely.

Ayden West: Okay, that's good.

My eyebrows met as I screwed up my face.

Effy Garcia: ???

Ayden West: Highly unlikely I can work with. It means I have a chance, no matter how small, I have a chance.

I sighed loudly wondering when he would realize how serious I was being.

Effy Garcia: Ayden, I am not changing my mind. I'm sorry.

Ayden West: I know, but I can't just sit back and not at least try.

Not wanting to argue, I replied *'okay'* and laid the phone beside me before its vibration shook the whole bed.

"Ayden?" I said, answering the phone.

"Good morning." he said cheerfully.

"Good morning." I replied, "Why are you calling me?"

"It's easier. Anyway, thanks to you, my mum has decided to throw me a birthday party."

"Hang on, why is that, one, a bad thing and two, my fault? Also, when is your birthday?" I asked, wondering why I didn't already know.

"One, it's a bad thing because parties arranged by mum normally end in her drunken antics, bringing it to a very early and dramatic ending and two, it's your fault, because you set her off on another attempt at sobriety. She wouldn't have even remembered my birthday, let alone throw a party if she was still drinking."

"Well, it sounds like I have actually done you a favour instead, and you didn't answer my question, when is your birthday?"

"Halloween."

"Oh, that explains so much." I laughed, "Please tell me this party involves Halloween costumes?"

"Getting a little ahead of yourself, aren't you? I haven't even invited you yet." He teased.

"With 'yet' being the operative word. Let's face it, you'd only spend the evening wishing I was there anyway."

He scoffed which I couldn't help but smile at.

"No chance. I am Ayden West, remember?"

I laughed out loud, "Oh sorry, Ayden West, please tell me, will I be honoured with an invitation?"

"That's more like it, but in all seriousness, yes, but you should know that my mum sent an invite to everyone at school…"

The smile on my face fell and instead replaced with irritation.

"Brogan."

"Yeah."

I wondered if it was a good idea if I went knowing she would try to cause trouble.

"I want you there, Annabella. If I have to, I will unin-vite her."

I sighed, "No, it'll just make me look petty. I'll be there, but I'll be covered head to toe in costume so she won't be able to find me. Fortunately for her, she won't need a costume seeing as she is already a demon." I snarled.

Ayden chuckled, "I'm glad you're coming."

"I'll let you know on the 1st of November if I feel the same."

He continued to chuckle, "I promise, it'll be worth it."

I rolled my eyes, glad that he couldn't see the big cheesy grin he was creating on my face.

"We'll see about that."

The day of Ayden's birthday party arrived and I had decided to dress up in the deathly colours of black and red, resembling La Catrina. Adding a large rose to the side of my face, I smiled back at my horrifying appearance. My eyes were masked with two black holes, surrounded by red gems that dazzled when they caught the light. My nose was also painted black to give the impression that it was no longer there but just a black hollow space. With cheekbones contoured in black and my lips covered with single black lines, I was ready.

"Well, look at you," Michael said from behind me, dressed in ripped clothes, a murky grey face with a knife going through his head.

"Thanks." I said patting down the multiple layers of colourful scratchy fabric that made up my skirt, "You look pretty impressive too — very zombie." I smiled although I wasn't sure if he could see any expression I made with the face paint I was wearing.

"Is Elizabeth coming?" I asked already knowing the answer after overhearing an argument between them.

"No." He shook his head, "But we won't let that spoil our fun."

I nodded before pulling on a pair of Effy's black heels and leaving the house with Michael.

We pulled up outside the hall with no doubts as to where the party was. Lit pumpkins and plastic gravestones were scattered outside with several black and orange balloons displaying the number 18.

"I wonder how Ayden's mum afforded all of this?" I asked, admiring the amount of detail that had been ensured as a vampire, a joker and two black cats walked in.

"Perhaps she got some help from someone..."

I looked over at Michael with raised eyebrows, "And I suppose you wouldn't know anything about who this 'someone' might be?"

He shrugged and smiled, "He deserves it and you know, it's the only eighteenth party I will get to throw." The sadness in his voice almost broke me in two.

"I'm sorry."

"Let's not worry about all that right now, Ayden will be here soon."

"What do you mean? Isn't he here already?"

Michael shook his head, "This was actually supposed to be a surprise party, but Ayden's mum couldn't keep it a secret. Anyway, we agreed we would at least surprise him with the effort. He'll be here soon." he finished, climbing out of the car.

We went past the hanging ghouls and cackling witches laughs and entered the hall, greeted by loud music played by a DJ in the corner of the hall filled with dancing teens and orange flashing lights amongst floating pumpkin lanterns.

"Wow, this is amazing," I said, noticing the smile on Michael's face before Ayden's mum ran over to us with opened arms and dressed as a wart-nosed witch.

"I was starting to think you wouldn't get here in time. Ayden is a few minutes away." she said excitedly before turning to face me and taking hold of my hands, "Effy, you probably know him best at the moment, do you think he'll like it?" The excitement had gone and was replaced with anxiety.

"Of course, Mrs. West. He will love it." I replied wondering if I really did know Ayden best.

"Great and it's Quinn to you... Oh, and I have someone that would like to meet you, Effy." she said as a little girl, almost hidden in an orange dress and pink fairy wings pulled at Quinn's leg.

She nervously smiled up at her mum as she played with the star on her yellow, sparkling wand.

"Kiah, this is Ayden's friend, Effy." I bent down so that she no longer had to look up at me and noticed the orange glitter on her eyes and the pink flowers in her hair.

"Hello, Fairy Kiah." She tilted her head and smiled playfully.

"Oh!" Quinn almost screamed as she received a text message, "I think he's here." she said, running over to the DJ and shushing everyone excitedly. It was great to see her so invested and so happy.

She soon joined us once again, holding her daughter's hand as Kiah looked up at me with a finger across her lips. I smiled and we all eagerly watched the entrance for Ayden to appear. I wondered what he would be dressed as and if he would act differently around me in the company of so many that knew him.

Soon my questions were answered and Ayden arrived to a roar of cheers, with a face painted as an incredibly realistic skeleton and dressed sharply in a well-fitted black suit that I couldn't help but admire him in. As he drank up the greetings from a crowd of creatures, I watched him carefully in what I assumed was his natural habitat at school. It was easy to forget that Ayden was the most popular boy in school when he made me feel like I was the only one that existed. His eyes flickered over to me, looking even more piercing than usual against the black painted around them. As he smiled at me, I was mesmerized by his jaw seeming to look sharper with the grey shadows.

He let go of his friends and made his way over to his mum, pulling her into a hug that sent her into the clouds or so you would have thought from the smile on her face.

"Thanks, mum." He smiled and I could tell he really meant it.

"Don't just thank me, Michael helped too. Seems you've made quite the impression with the Garcia family." She smiled at Michael and I swear I saw the slightest blush.

"Oh really, it's nothing, it was all your mum's idea, I just hung the really heavy stuff." He laughed as Quinn squeezed his arm.

"Thanks, Michael, I really appreciate it," Ayden said giving him a manly hug.

"No trouble at all, my boy."

"Right, well, why don't we get ourselves a drink, Quinn..." Michael's eyes shot open and his cheeks flushed red as he realised what he had said, "...a drink of water or coke, perhaps, I'm driving, you see." he spluttered causing us to laugh.

"Oh Michael, you do make me laugh." she said, pulling him off and leaving Ayden and me.

"Is it just me or were they flirting?" Ayden laughed.

"Somehow that wouldn't be the worst thing in the world," I replied, keeping my gaze on them at the bar ordering water, unable to shrug the nerves I currently had.

"You look incredible by the way, those stockings are really doing things for you." He smirked as he admired my legs.

"Yes, well, I had to make sure I stood out so that you didn't lose me in the crowd."

He smirked and raised his hand to my cheek to brush away a hair that had fallen loose. He stepped closer causing my breathing to become shaky as he tucked the hair behind my ear and whispered, "I find it fascinating how you think you could be lost in a crowd, dressed up or not."

I smiled and shrugged, "I guess I'm just grateful I got an invite."

Ayden laughed as he shook his head before placing his hand on the bottom of my back, "Come on, I want you to meet my family."

We spent the next few hours chatting to his brothers who had returned to London for Ayden's party, watching his uncle pull some questionable shapes on the dance floor and played and won a game of beer pong that left me feeling fuzzy.

Already feeling as if the room was spinning, I found a quiet table in the corner of the hall where all the empty or abandoned cups had been left. I watched how the party guests who had started the evening in their own little groups were now, thanks to a steady supply of alcohol, dancing and chatting away with anyone they set eyes on. It was my favourite part of a party, when all judgements and caution had been thrown to the wind and groups came together. It was something that hadn't changed much over the years.

Unable to see Ayden amongst the crowds, I found Michael being forced to dance with Ayden's mum and one of his aunts I could no longer remember the name of. It was the first time I had seen him so relaxed and at ease despite being out of his comfort zone. I wondered for a moment whether there could be potential for him and Ayden's mum. It's not as though his marriage with Elizabeth was made to last and Ayden's mum deserved someone stable in her life.

"Oh dear." I stiffened as I heard the two words fall out of the mouth of Brogan. Sighing, I turned to find her standing in between Jessica and Naomi. I couldn't help but notice how pretty Brogan looked as a broken doll in a short chequered doll's dress and her Auburn hair tied up in pigtails. Jessica and Naomi had both dressed up as zombie cheerleaders with blood splashed up their arms and across their faces.

"You would have thought today would have been easy for you given how you naturally look and yet you still get it so miserably wrong." Brogan scoffed, waiting for the girls to laugh, but only Naomi did.

"What? I actually think she looks good." Jessica smiled

at me which I returned quickly before Brogan rolled her eyes.

"I'm sorry, Jessica, should I leave you here with your new best friend or are you going to shut that dumb mouth of yours?" I watched as Jessica's eyes fell to the ground and her shoulders sunk.

"What are you even doing here? Desperately hoping Ayden will finally notice you?" Brogan spoke with words laced with poison.

"Brogan— " I sighed and stood up before being cut off.

"Do you not ever get tired of being a bitch all the time?" Ayden spoke from beside me as we watched Brogan's mouth almost hit the floor beside a wide-eyed Naomi and a hidden smirk from Jessica.

"It's my birthday, Brogan. Please, go dance, have some fun and leave my girlfriend alone."

I was too busy to notice their reactions as I was far more caught up in my own, but I could imagine the word 'girl-friend' had created a similar effect on us all.

Did he say girlfriend? *I think he did. Had we agreed to that? Had I missed a conversation?*

"Come on, let's go." Ayden smiled, taking my hand into his own and pulling me away through the crowd of dancers into the middle of the dance floor as people squeezed his shoulder and sent him cheesy grins and thumbs ups.

"You said girlfriend," I said, standing completely still except for a raised brow and a scrunched up nose.

"Yeah..." he said casually dancing.

"But I'm not... right?" I said, trying really hard to remember if I had completely missed this important conversation.

Ayden laughed cooly, "No. I figured it would help keep Brogan at bay. Like stunning a fish."

"Right... but you do realise that this will spread like wildfire and people will think we are together?"

He shrugged, "So what?"

A smile grew on my face before I began to chuckle completely lost for words.

"What's so funny?"

"You, this, all of it." I smiled and took a well-needed breath as I stared into his perfect eyes. I couldn't tell whether it was the alcohol or adrenaline, but I stepped closer to him and held onto to his black tie, revelling in his musky scent. He remained still, seeming as cool as possible as I leant in and rested my forehead against his, placing my hand around his neck and closing my eyes.

"I've never met anyone like you, Ayden," I whispered.

Without saying a word, Ayden's warm lips were on mine and the rest of the world seemed to fall away. The kiss was slow, saying all the things our words wouldn't.

As he let out a low moan, I pulled away noticing the black lines on his mouth had smudged into a foggy cloud. With my heart racing, I looked around to find no one had spotted us, well at least no one that was still looking. I grabbed Ayden's hand and pulled him through the crowds to what I had thought was a fire exit, but was a door to a narrow and dark corridor. I pushed the door shut behind us and quickly pushed Ayden against the wall, wanting to tear away every layer of fabric that was on him.

"Well, this is new." He smirked before I forced my lips onto his. Kissing him obliterated every thought, worry and concern and added to a blazing fire spreading through me.

Kissing me just as furiously, Ayden bent low, scooped up my legs and pushed me into the opposite wall. He laced my neck with kisses that caused the hair on my arms to stand tall as I leant my head back against the wall, completely breathless in delight. Spotting another door at the end of the corridor, I held Ayden's face in my hands and whispered, "Wait, where's that door lead to?"

He looked over at it before letting go of me and walking over to the door.

"How much are we hoping it's a bedroom with a lock?" He laughed as he took hold of the handle. I gently hit his arm as I stood beside him, silently wishing the same thing.

Ayden opened the door quickly to display a room filled with packed shelves and clutter.

"A storage room." I laughed.

"Yes, but one with a lock," Ayden smirked, pointing at a lock on the door that would only need a strong breeze to force it open.

"One of two is better than nothing." I shrugged before pushing the door shut and carefully locking it.

As I turned back to face Ayden, he took my face into his hands and began to kiss me. Feeling less self-conscious, I began to pull off his suit jacket and loosen his tie whilst his hands moved down my back, finding the zip to the dress. Quickly and with ease, he spun me around so that I faced the door as he slowly began to unzip the dress. It eventually fell to the floor just as every little care I had would when I was around Ayden.

Lying on the floor, surrounded by clutter that had fallen during our time in the storage room, I leant on my side, resting my head on Ayden's bare chest.

"I wish I didn't have to leave," I whispered and even though I knew he would have thought I meant leaving the room, I was talking about it all.

"I'm sure there will be plenty of opportunities for a repeat." He winked, "I can't believe the 'girlfriend' tactic worked so well."

I slapped his chest causing him to chuckle, "I'm joking, kind of." He smirked before tilting his head down to kiss me.

Enjoying the moment of being in his arms and tracing the shadows on his chest, I thought about the next five months. I knew one thing for sure, I wanted to be with Ayden in every and any way possible, but I also wanted it to be memorable, not just for me but for him too. I wanted to live in his memories forever.

I rolled onto my elbows and looked up at his peaceful face, looking up at the ceiling.

"Ayden, I want to spend the next few months having fun, exploring and trying new things and I want to do that with you, if you want."

He slowly wiggled up, resting his head on a beaten cardboard box that wouldn't have surprised me if it was filled with dead rats.

"That goes without saying. What did you have in mind? I say it involves lots of that 'angry Annabella' that pushed me against a wall and ripped my clothes off." He gave a suggestive look.

I rolled my eyes and laughed, "Blame the beer pong."

"Never! But let's also add lots of beer pong to the list."

I shook my head, resisting the temptation to kiss him.

"The last few decades, I've really not tried to enjoy myself or try anything new and I want to start now."

Ayden nodded, "We'll do anything you want. You name it and we'll try to make it happen."

"Okay." I smiled looking at his smudged skeleton face that he still managed to make look good. "You know, you're not horrible to look at."

"Oh, I'm not am I?" Ayden grinned mischievously.

"Try not letting your head get any bigger otherwise we'll struggle to squeeze it out of this room."

"Well, for what it's worth, you're not so bad to look at, too."

I smiled weakly and rested my head on his arm.

"Did I say something wrong?" Ayden said in a more serious voice, sitting up and forcing me to sit up too.

"Yes... No..." I let out a sigh as he watched me carefully, "It's just I look like Effy, it's not me."

He softly smiled and took my hand, stopping me from picking at my nails, "Annabella, I don't know how to say this in a way that you'll believe me or in a way that'll make sense, but it's different somehow. I knew Effy, I had the opportunity to go there with her and whilst she was a pretty girl, I wasn't really interested. Since you arrived, Effy hasn't looked like Effy. I don't see you as her anymore. Even before we knew who you were and before I even knew the truth, you were always different."

I nodded and grinned, "That was a pretty good answer."

He shrugged, "What can I say? I'm the total package." He laughed before I climbed onto his lap and began our mission of fun.

Chapter ELEVEN

I n none of my previous lives had I ever complained of time going by too quickly and never could I imagine myself doing so, but as I crossed off the final day in February, I found myself wishing it would all slow down a little bit.

How could it be March already?

The last few months since Ayden's birthday had been nothing short of amazing as we spent every possible minute together doing all the things we both wanted to do. We had visited theme parks where plenty of teddy bears had been won and I had been dragged on every rollercoaster that Ayden had set his eyes on. We also went to the theatre to see shows I hadn't seen for years and Ayden had never seen. Afterwards, we would have picnics or sit in a fast food car park snacking on burgers. Christmas and New Year soon arrived and we celebrated together. Michael had persuaded Elizabeth to invite Ayden and his family to join us on Christmas Day for dinner. Both Michael and I could see how much it meant to Ayden's mum as she watched Ayden and his siblings relax and enjoy the day. Ayden's family joined us once again for the New Years Eve party Elizabeth had arranged. It was strange celebrating the festive season in the way that I had as Effy when so many before had been very different. No gift sharing, no board games after overeating on far too many roasted potatoes and definitely none of the perfect family moments I had shared with both Effy and Ayden's families. But as the clocks struck for the new year, I was met with the familiar feeling of dread as the days begun to fall away fast.

Ayden and I hadn't really talked about what was to come. It was either bad timing on my part or Ayden would quickly change the subject. I knew that no matter the number of times I tried to remind him, he was hopeful I would change my mind which was becoming more and more tempting, but when I reminded myself why, I knew my mind was made up.

We had one last trip planned that I had taken the liberty to arrange and surprise Ayden with. After days of dodging his questions and hiding the details, we finally arrived in Madrid, Spain on a fairly warm Saturday morning.

"I cannot believe we're in Spain. I've barely been out of London, let alone a foreign country!" Ayden said excitedly as we checked into our hotel.

"Well, the surprises don't stop here. In fact, we don't have long before we have to leave again, so you may want to get washed up and ready soon."

"You're amazing." he said before he squished my cheeks together and kissed me.

I smiled as he walked off into the bathroom unable to shift the churning feeling in my stomach. I walked out onto the small balcony and took a deep breath of the Spanish air and the view of a busy street filled with people going about their Saturday. I pulled my phone out of my pocket and found a few text messages, two from Michael wishing us a good trip and asking if we had landed. There was another from Aniya which had been dictated to her daughter.

. . .

Aniya: Good, then I will come the day before so I can prepare. It's a complex soul jump, so it'll have to be somewhere I can harvest enough power. I have contacts nearby you that will be able to help me find the right place. I'll contact you a few days beforehand.

Effy Garcia: Do you need me to do anything?

I replied knowing it would be a little while until she messaged me back. I locked the phone and placed it back in my pocket as Ayden returned into the room.

"So, where are we going next?"

We climbed into a taxi as Ayden went through a list of things he thought we might be doing.

"Is it Spanish related?" he asked.

"Yes."

"Is it an activity?"

"Yes, but not physical for us."

I watched his face screw up, "I just don't know what it could be."

"Look out of the window," I said nudging his arm as we arrived outside of the Bernabeu Stadium.

Ayden's head spun back so fast I was worried it may go all the way around.

"No way? You got us tickets to a Real Madrid game?" he said like a child just told they were going to Disneyland.

"I kind of did." I smiled, pulling out two tickets for the game that he immediately snatched before planting a slightly painful kiss in between my mouth and cheek.

We hurried out of the car and made our way inside for the game where Real Madrid won the match 3-0 providing Ayden with plenty of content to spend the next few hours during dinner commentating on.

"I'm sorry, I must be boring you now." he paused mid-dissecting a free kick that led to one of the goals.

I gently laughed, "No, not at all, it's nice to see you so passionate, even if it *is* football."

"I never in a million years thought I would get to see them play. You've honestly made a dream of mine come true." he said squeezing my hand.

I smiled back, trying to ignore the guilt I felt knowing already he had never been to a game before and using it to my advantage, knowing that every time he would think about it, he would remember me.

As we decided to walk back to our hotel from the restaurant, we watched the sunset in a spectacular array of orange and reds. Once darkness had arrived, so too did the nightlife of Madrid as the bars began to fill with people beginning their pre-drinks of Sangria, dancing away to the Latin music.

"Have you ever lived in Spain?" Ayden asked as we walked hand in hand down a narrow street filled with vibrant bars.

"I did, I think about seventeen different times. My favourite was Sofia Martinez." I smiled fondly.

"She sounds hot."

I laughed as I rolled my eyes, "She was. One second..." I said pulling my phone out and typing her name into Google, ignoring the reports of her death and finding what I was looking for.

"Look..." I said, showing him a video of a beautiful brunette with the fullest smile and perfect almond shaped eyes take the stage with a male partner.

"You were a dancer?" Ayden said with his eyes lighting up as Sofia began to dance.

"Yes, well, she was. In fact, she was one of the best.

Here, this was me dancing the Lambada, the forbidden dance." I remembered.

"This doesn't look so long ago." He pointed out, but not taking his eyes from the video playing on my screen.

"No, it was in 1997. It was a good life."

"I bet." he said before looking up in front of him and then shifting his gaze to me with a smirk.

"What?" I asked.

"Let's go dance."

I laughed until I realised he was being serious, "No, don't be silly. I'm not even sure I could even do that in this body."

He shook his head and began to lead me to one of the loud bars playing Spanish music, "Come on, we are here in Spain, the night is young and I really want to see you dance."

"Ayden, seriously, I don't think I even know how to dance like that anymore. It was such a long time ago."

"I bet it's like riding a bike and plus I'm sure Michael is Spanish, so you have some of Effy's Spanish blood in you."

"Yes, I'm sure that is how it works, Ayden, Spanish blood means being able to dance..."

He shrugged, "Come on, we are here to have fun, right?"

I rolled my eyes and sighed as I followed him into the bar, immediately greeted by the staff with a shot of tequila.

"Salud!" they shouted in chorus over the loud music.

I grimaced at the taste before declining another.

"Okay, go dance!" Ayden said pushing me away.

"You are dancing with me..." I pulled at his hand, but he didn't budge.

"No chance after seeing you dance in that video."

"Well, I can't dance alone." I returned to the bar, trying to gain the attention of the barman for a drink.

"Then dance with him." Ayden pointed out a man dressed in a white shirt with far too many buttons open.

"No."

Ayden ignored me, hopping off the stool and walking over to the man as they both looked over to me and smiled.

If this man comes over, I will strangle you, Ayden... Please, don't come over.

With my hopes being ignored, Ayden walked over with his new friend in tow.

"Hola, me llamo Sergio. Your amigo tells me you like to dance the forbidden dance."

I shook my head with a strained smile, "Oh no, he has it wrong, I can't dance."

Sergio laughed and flipped his dark, greasy locks back revealing a damp, sweaty forehead.

"I don't believe you. Now, come! We must dance." he said, pulling me into the centre of the room despite my resistance.

I sighed as he ordered for the DJ to play the Lambada, but I couldn't help but smile once the song began to play, reminded by the days of Sofia Martinez. As Sergio placed his leg in between mine, he held my hand out and placed his other on the small of my back before we began to sway our hips left to right, moving across the floor as though it belonged to us. At first, I played along, making half an effort to take part, but as the song played on and the crowd on the dance floor cleared to watch, I found myself enjoying it. Quickly, he bent me back causing my hair to come loose and pulled me back up to send me off in a twirl.

The crowd was now watching, clapping away with the beat, including Ayden, who watched with a huge grin.

Sergio and I moved around in sync as though we had been dancing for years as my dress twirled and my hair followed.

Once the song came to an end, the crowd roared with applause and Sergio bent on one knee to kiss my hand, "Oh, Annabella, you dance like no one I have ever danced with. I could dance with you forever." he said and I smiled pulling him up onto his feet before giving him a quick hug.

I returned back to Ayden who slowly clapped until I reached him and swatted his hands.

"That. Was. The hottest thing I have ever seen." He laughed.

"Oh stop it, can we go now?" I blushed, pulling at him to leave.

"How about we go back and you show me a few more of those moves tonight?" he said with raised eyebrows.

"You are disgusting." I laughed.

Once we reached the hotel, Ayden suggested that we sit on the balcony and enjoy the cool evening, watching the busy street.

"Yes, good idea, but let me shower first. Every time Real Madrid scored, I was covered in splatters of beer and after all that dancing, I have this kind of sweaty, beer smell going on." I shuddered.

"Sexy." Ayden winked as I walked into the bathroom.

I climbed into the shower and allowed the warm water to wash away the day's dirt, wishing it would also take away the permanent dread and guilt I felt.

I had experienced so many things over the past 109 years, but nothing compared to this. I knew I was making the right decision, but it didn't mean I was completely convinced I wanted to go through with it.

Standing in front of the foggy mirror, I looked back at Effy's reflection knowing I would also have to speak to

Michael too. We both knew I was nothing like the real Effy, but we also knew that I was still some comfort to Michael, he still got to see Effy smile and laugh. I wondered how he would cope.

"That's it, Annabella. You've got to stop this." I whispered to the reflection.

"We've got 27 days before this all comes to an end, we're doing the right thing, so stop wasting time thinking about it all and just enjoy the days we have left, okay?" I finished half expecting Effy's reflection to reply.

I picked up a towel and wrapped it around me before leaving the bathroom to join Ayden. He was sat on the balcony as promised. As I walked out to join him, I squeezed his shoulder, "Still thinking about the game?" I said, immediately dropping my smile, noticing his posture stiffen at my touch. He didn't move, but kept his gaze on the building opposite.

"Is everything alright?" I asked before he reached his arm out and handed me my phone. My stomach sunk and without him saying a word more, I knew what he had seen. With no time to scorn myself, Ayden spoke, "I can't believe it."

"I'm sorry, Ayden," I said looking down at the message sent from Aniya.

Aniya: You don't need to do anything, but start saying your goodbyes.

"I can't believe you lied to me." My eyes shot over to Ayden as he stood up and began to walk back into the room.

"Lied to you? When did I lie to you?"

"This whole time, you've led me to believe that you weren't going to go ahead with it."

I laughed in dismay, "Are you being serious? These past five months, all I have tried to do is be honest with you, but you never let me. You always create some sort of distraction or change the subject! So don't you dare tell me that I lied to you. I told you from day one I was going ahead with this."

"Then why are you sorry?" He stared back at me.

"Ayden, I'm not sorry that I'm going to do it, I'm sorry because I know you don't want me to. The last five months have been a chance for us to enjoy each other's company and do things we have always wanted to do before our time was up."

"So you used me?"

I shook my head in disbelief and looked away, "I'm not even going to answer that question, because if you don't already know the answer to it then there is no point in me wasting my breath."

Silence fell in the room as I walked out onto the balcony as Ayden sat on the bed. Feeling my hands tremble from a mixture of the cool air against the bare parts of my skin not covered by the towel and a rage of anger, I held onto the balcony to steady myself.

"Why are you giving up?"

"What am I giving up, Ayden?" I said walking back into the room.

"The chance to live, the chance to be with me."

"You don't get it, this isn't some sort of incredible miracle. I am stuck as a 17-year-old. I can't get married, I can't have children, I can't buy a house or even do the lottery." I paused and slowly shook my head as Ayden's gaze fell to the floor.

"I am not living, I am just existing as a stranger for 364

days a year before I go onto the next. What happens if in the next life I am a boy and live in the middle of nowhere with no way of getting back to you? Then what, Ayden? Are you going to wait another year and hope I become a girl again? And what happens when years down the line when you are no longer interested in me, because you're in your twenties or thirties and I am still 17 years old? Then what, Ayden? I'll tell you what, I'll be left alone, having lost the one opportunity I had to no longer feel trapped whilst you go and live your life." I was shouting now, unable to fight the angry tears rolling down my face.

Ayden shook his head, "So you expect me to just accept it? Accept that in a few weeks, you will be gone forever?"

"I don't expect you to do anything, but I'm sorry Ayden, it's happening whether you accept it or not.

His jaw tightened as his eyes began to glisten, "Well I want you to know, if you go ahead with this, I won't be there or have any part to play in this suicide mission. If you tell me right now that this is really going to happen then this is it, I never want to see you again."

His words hit me in the chest like a knife to the lungs, robbing me of breathe and leaving me with an ache that spread across me like a raging fire. I closed my eyes to soothe the sting, wishing I had taken my phone into the bathroom with me.

I opened my eyes releasing a flood of tears and looked up at him, waiting for an answer I couldn't give him. I stepped closer to him and leaned forward, placing a kiss on his cheek before whispering, "I'm sorry, Ayden."

Feeling slightly grateful for not having unpacked already, I picked up my small suitcase and walked out of the room, leaving Ayden and Madrid behind me.

The next few days seemed to drag endlessly as I waited for Michael to return from his trip to a teacher's training camp. For most of the day, I would sleep, only waking to use the toilet and during the night, I would lie awake thinking about my decision, Ayden and Michael. I hated how unfair it was to have my last life be one of the very few lives I didn't want to end when so many had been so rubbish. I hated how this life had to be the life that I fell for Ayden West.

When Michael finally arrived, he knew straight away something was wrong as he knocked on my door to find me lying in darkness.

"What has happened? I tried to call Ayden, but he isn't answering my calls. So I spoke to Quinn and she told me how Ayden won't talk to her and has rarely left his room. What is going on?" he said with a face full of concern.

I climbed off the bed for the first time in hours and ran into his arms, comforted by his smell.

"What has happened?"

"I told him I was going to go ahead with Aniya, so we broke up." I looked up at him feeling the sting in my eyes.

"Oh, my love." he said, squeezing me tighter, "Don't worry, he will come back. He's just hurting."

"No, I don't think he will. He asked me to choose and said that if I went ahead with it, he didn't want to see me anymore."

"Please don't cry. I'll see if I can talk to him."

"No. I don't want you to. I have hurt him enough,

there's no need to carry on." I looked up at Michael once again, "Will you be there with me on the day? I don't want to be alone when it happens."

He smiled, but I could see how hard it was for him to answer, "I wouldn't dream of being anywhere else in the world."

Chapter
TWELVE

The final few days of my last life as Effy Garcia was approaching quicker than I had wanted and as the 28th arrived, I laid awake all night until morning had arrived, not catching a wink of sleep.

I hadn't spoken to Ayden since Madrid, not even Michael had heard from him. I didn't expect either of us would. At least, I knew I wouldn't.

Aniya had called the previous night to let me know she was prepared to go ahead for the next day and decided that the best place to garner the power she needed was an underground tomb in a cemetery nearby. It was a tomb belonging to one of the leaders of Shal Vida's.

"I know it sounds incredibly frightening, but he was a strong man and has all the power I will need to perform the jump." she assured.

I climbed out of the bed and pulled out one of the many untouched notebooks Effy had owned. Inside, I began to write a letter to Ayden.

Dear Ayden,

By the time that you read this, I will be gone. It's insane that I am even able to write that sentence when I thought this would be the way I lived forever.

I'm sorry that I have put you through all of this and

included you in this mess, but I am not sorry for meeting you. I'm not sorry for getting to know you and I am not sorry for falling for you.

I want you to know that even though I decided to go ahead with this, you made it so difficult to actually do it when just last year I would have never even had a second thought. You were the reasons for my doubts.

This past year has been the best life I have ever lived and trust me, I know by now what makes a life good. It's waking up knowing you are important to someone, whether that be your friend or your father. Knowing that someone chooses to spend their time with you, wanting to make memories that you can both share. It's about laughter and tears, about happiness and sadness. It's about being able to leave this world knowing you truly lived and not just existed and that's what you helped me do. I know you will probably never understand why I made this decision and in your eyes, it may seem like I gave up, but I didn't. I just knew I would never enjoy a life better than I had this one and what better way to end it than knowing I had spent it with you.

One day, I hope you will learn to forgive me and move on to someone who perhaps deserves you more than I did but until then, I want you to know that you are the most caring person I have ever met. The way you just believed my story, even though it was insane, you trusted me with no hesitation. You are a beautiful soul that has so much good to look forward to, I just hope you don't hold yourself back in fear of someone seeing the real 'you'.

If my time with you has taught me anything, it's that time is precious and life shouldn't be taken for granted no matter how many shots you get at it.

Remember me.

Annabella x

. . .

I folded the letter in half and tucked it into an envelope before walking downstairs to Michael. He was stood in the kitchen by the sink staring out of a window that led out onto the garden.

I took the last step on the stairs with a little extra force causing him to come out of his daze and continue cleaning the sides. Ever since discovering who I really was, I had felt uncomfortable calling Michael 'dad' and so I had stopped. He had also stopped calling me Effy. Instead, we wouldn't use any names at all, but use other subtle gestures to get each other's attention. I knew he would never be ready to let Effy go no matter how ready I was to let her go.

"How are you feeling?" he said as I sat down at the counter.

"Every kind of emotion possible, you?"

He dropped the cloth into the sink and looked up at me, "I have no idea."

I nodded and began to pick at the splinters of wicker basket holding fruit, "The house has been quiet lately."

"She's left," Michael replied knowing what I had meant. As time grew closer, Michael began to argue back each time Elizabeth snapped at him until he reached a breaking point and told her he wanted a divorce. I'm not entirely sure he did actually want to separate from her or if it was just a tactic to get her to realise how unhappy he was, but either way, she left without a fight and hadn't returned.

"I know," I replied as I accidentally caught my finger with a single splinter from the basket. We sat in silence as I sat and watched a tiny pool of blood collect at the tip of my finger.

"Are you sure you're going to be alright coming with me tonight?"

He sighed out loud, rubbing his unshaven ash coloured stubble, "Honestly, I don't know anymore. It was one thing to be losing Effy, but now I've lost my wife... I just don't know anymore."

"I understand." I said walking around the kitchen counter and squeezing his hands, "I can do this alone." I lied and he nodded.

"Can I ask for just one favour?" I asked.

"Of course."

"Effy had a savings account she couldn't touch until she was 18, right?" I had recalled it from an entry in her diary where she went on to list the things she wanted to do with it.

"Yes, she did... she still has." Michael looked at me curiously.

"One of the ways she said she wanted to use it was to help people and I wondered if you would let me give some of it away to help someone." I felt rude for asking, knowing full well I had no right, but even after a divorce, I knew Michael would be fine financially.

"To give to who?"

"Ayden and his mum. I feel like she is more than ready to live her life differently now and I want Ayden to have some so that he can start his life properly."

He didn't reply, but looked deep in thought.

"I mean, I completely understand if you don't agree..."

"No, I do. They deserve a break and it's not like I'll need it. Leave it with me, I'll make sure they are okay."

I exhaled contently, knowing that there was only one thing left that I had to do before it was time to go.

I thanked Michael and excused myself back to Effy's bedroom.

Sitting on the bed were several boxes filled with a variety of Effy's belongings and I had written notes on each for Michael to find once I had gone. On a box filled with her clothes, I had told Michael to keep a few items but donate the rest. On a box filled with her accessories and jewellery, I told him to take the valuables and also donate the rest, reminding him that she would always live far longer in his memories than the items would. I had boxed up her school books and asked that he throw it away. Finally, I had one box left to fill. First, I picked up the photos of her that I had taken from her phone and had printed to add to the box, knowing it was unlikely Michael had ever seen them. Next, I picked up a heart shaped photo frame that Effy had left on her bedside table of her and Michael and placed it inside. I continued to fill the box with items I had discovered over the year that I thought Effy may want her dad to keep before moving on to her diary. I had read every single page filled with Effy's happiness and sadness. From the moments she began to grow unhappy up until her final days. I knew I was going to leave Michael the diary, but what had troubled me for weeks had been the question of whether I should leave him the suicide note too. I had read it a million times, so much so that I could recite it whilst trying to figure out if Michael needed to see it until I realised it wasn't really my decision.

I picked up the letter, slotting it between the pages of the diary before setting the book down in the box and began writing my final note.

This is Effy's diary and inside is her suicide note. I should have given it to you sooner and I am sorry for keeping it from you. I won't lie to you and say it's filled with happy memories, because it isn't. It has the raw moments of pain she felt and her deepest worries and concerns, but I am not giving this to you so that you can focus on the negative parts. I am leaving it here for you to have so you can see that whilst she was unhappy with so much in her life, you were never the reason why. Whilst I never got to meet the real Effy, it wasn't difficult to see just how much she loved you. I hope this helps you to see that and that one day you learn how to stop blaming yourself for her death. From the moment I met you, I knew you were special and until we met Aniya, I couldn't put my finger on it until I remembered who I was and I realised that you were just like my own father. Thank you for letting me feel that love one last time.

So from both Effy and I, we ask that you remember to live once in a while and show the world just how much of an amazing person you are.

With all my love
Annabella x

I wiped my damp face and folded the note in half before sticking it to the front of the diary. Slowly, I closed the final box and looked around the room that had been home for the past 364 days.

I really couldn't believe it would be all over soon.

Taking a deep breath in hope of delaying the tears, I took one last look before leaving the room and closing the door behind me. As I walked down the corridor, I recalled the first day I had woken as Effy and was greeted by the very same pictures currently hanging on the wall. I had no idea what they would become to me. I had no idea how important this life would really be.

As I reached the kitchen, I found Michael waiting at the bottom of the stairs for me. I took one look at his face and had to force my eyes shut to stop myself from breaking down.

"Let's not make this any harder than it has to be, okay?" he spoke slowly, but it didn't stop his voice from shaking.

I nodded and bit on my bottom lip, "Alright, but I just want to say..." I paused to try and compose myself knowing it would be impossible, "thank you so much for believing me and taking me in just as you would have with Effy. I will forever be in your debt."

Michael reached out and pulled me into his chest one last time as I allowed myself to sob, "Thank you for giving me more time with my little girl. For that, I will forever be in your debt."

He placed a kiss on my forehead before squeezing me one last time and walked away.

I left the house, finding Aniya and her daughter in a car ready to pick me up. Climbing inside, Aniya nodded at me with a smile worth a thousand embraces as I settled into the back seat only thinking of how much I wanted to say goodbye to Ayden.

We soon arrived in the middle of a dark forest where Aniya led the way with an old-fashioned hand lantern.

"I'm sorry we have to take this route, but we wouldn't be granted access to the cemetery at this time." she spoke amongst the sound of the twigs crunching beneath us.

We soon arrived at the entrance of the brick tomb that Aniya had described. To say it was creepy was a complete understatement as old and broken tombs laid scattered around with the sound of rats scuttling in the background.

Aniya's daughter pushed opened the tomb door

revealing a set of very dark stairs only faintly lit by Aniya's light.

"Don't worry, there is plenty of light downstairs. We came earlier to set up."

I followed behind and soon discovered the room Aniya was talking about. It was a lot bigger than I had imagined, with dust and dirt living in every possible corner. Scattered around were hundreds of candles keeping the room lit in an orange blaze.

"Before we begin, I need to ask one final time, are you sure you want to do this, Annabella?"

It was a question I had asked myself a million times and no matter how many reasons I had to not go ahead with it, I had the one reason why I should do it, which outweighed it all.

I nodded, "I'm sure."

"Ok, then I need you to please lie down on this tomb. I know it may feel slightly strange, but it is best that you are as close as you can be to our leader."

I took one look at the old tomb stood in the middle of the room and shivered, "No, it's not strange at all." I hesitated.

Aniya's daughter helped me climb on to the large piece of concrete holding the skeleton of the man that would help me become the very same.

"Are you okay, my dear?" Aniya asked.

"As okay as I will ever be," I said lying down, forcing myself to become comfortable on the hard and cold platform.

"Let me explain what will happen. Soon, I will begin the ritual and you will feel tired. You need to give in to the tiredness and allow your dreams to take over. You'll then wake in what will feel like a dream, but it won't be. This will be where you have to do your part. You will be at the bridge where you last jumped and once you hear the clock begin, wait for its eleventh chime and then you must jump."

"What happens then?" I asked.

"Then my dear, you will finally be at peace."

"Okay." I nodded feeling the nervousness shoot through me as I grew moments away from the end, "Aniya, am I doing the right thing?"

She looked down at me with a smile, "Only you know if you are ready, my child. What you have to ask yourself is whether you are prepared to wake up as someone else tomorrow."

I felt her squeeze my hand as I used the other to wipe a tear away. It was everything I had said to Ayden. I did want to stay for him and for Michael, but when the clock struck midnight, I wouldn't be Effy Garcia again and I didn't want to be anyone else. I was Annabella Hart who was supposed to have died over a hundred years ago. I had long overstayed my welcome and I was tired.

I was so tired.

"I wish they were here, Aniya." I broke a little.

She nodded, "I know my dear, but you know better than most how to be strong on your own."

"Thank you for helping me, Aniya." I smiled.

"It's been a pleasure, Annabella."

I took a look around at the underground tomb, noticing the little webs in the corners highlighted by the candlelight.

This was it. My final place. *My final life.*

"Are you ready?"

I bit my lip hard and whispered, "Okay..." before Aniya nodded. She lowered over me and brushed away the hair from my face.

"When you are ready, close your eyes and allow the tiredness to take you."

I took a deep breath, feeling my hands tremble beside me before closing my eyes.

"Wait!" A voice echoed through the tomb, causing both Aniya and I to jump. I sat up and watched the entrance, waiting for the voice to appear.

"Annabella..." the voice called, followed by Michael looking frantic.

"Michael?" I climbed off the platform and hurried over to him.

"Sorry... I tracked your phone and found you here." he said trying to gain his breath. "I was selfish before, you need me to be here and that is what I'm going to do, no matter how hard it is."

I nodded, feeling the tears rolling down my face before pulling him into a hug.

"I would really like that," I replied, enjoying the momentary feeling of safety I felt when in his arms.

I had learned over the years that some people became parents the day their child arrived into the world, but there were a few that were *made* to be parents, and Michael was one of them. I just wished it wasn't him who had to suffer.

"Annabella..." Aniya called, pulling me out of the moment with Michael, "we should begin, it's almost midnight."

I looked over at her and nodded before squeezing Michael's hands, "Thank you for being here."

I walked back to the platform and laid down, once again, feeling the cold seep through my clothes to my skin, causing a chill to rush through me. I knew it wouldn't be long before I would begin the process of leaving the body. It was a feeling I had come to terms with a long time ago. The feeling of losing all breath as though my lungs were about to burst. The blood in my veins rushing through me to my heart, causing it to race and the feeling of knowing I would wake up soon enough as somebody else. I didn't ever want to feel that again.

"It's time," I whispered, smiling at Michael, who stood in the corner trying to hide his lone tear.

Aniya began to brush the hair away from my face once again before whispering, "Close your eyes and allow yourself to sleep one last time, Annabella."

I did as she said and began to feel the drowsiness slip in, just as it would at the hospital preparing for an operation. In the background, I could faintly hear Aniya beginning to chant in a language I had never heard in any lifetime and the occasional sniffle from Michael.

Visions soon began to fill the darkness, images of my previous lives flashed by, all in order, starting with my first. Moments of both good and bad memories rushed past... Hannah George, Kadir Mostafa, Jerry Leroy, Alice Temple... so many lives and so many memories and then finally, the last one appeared.

Effy Garcia.

I have to lived over a hundred lifetimes, but only this one really mattered.

Chapter THIRTEEN

AYDEN

I had tried my best all day to ignore it, but as the time neared midnight, I couldn't focus on anything but the date.

I was still so angry at her for choosing to leave, even though I understood why she had to. Just because she was ready to let go, didn't mean I was. I wanted so much more.

I pulled out my phone and looked at the text message from Michael for what had been the thousandth time.

Don't let your stubbornness and pride get in the way of allowing yourself the opportunity to say goodbye. You will only live a lifetime with regret once she is gone. She'll be at the old Limestone Cemetery — enter from the forest side.

Throwing myself back onto the bed, I pictured her face and the way her smile would light up a room. She had single-handedly changed my life forever; helping my mum to really try and change, taking me places I never thought I would see and teaching me how to be happy again. I needed to see her. I needed to tell her how thankful I was.

"I need to go," I said out loud to an empty bedroom before throwing on my shoes and racing outside.

The forest wasn't too far away from me, at most ten minutes away. I checked the time to find it was 11.52pm.

I ran as quickly as I could, pushing past the gradual ache in my lungs and legs, knocking anyone in my way to one side.

All I could think about was seeing her. How could I have been so stupid? I hadn't deserved her at all.

Racing through the forest and almost tripping several times from the dizziness, I could finally make out the entrance of the tomb in the darkness. I could feel my heart's rapid beat shaking my skull as my vision became blurry.

"Annabella!" I yelled as loud as I could as I reached the entrance and raced down the stairs, tumbling into the room to find her lying still.

"No..." I whispered, holding on to the rough wall as though my consciousness relied on it. Beside me stood Michael, crying silently as Aniya stood over her body.

"Annabella...?" I called, but she didn't move. I could see the usual rosy pink in her cheeks beginning to fade, replaced with a grey mask. The frown on her forehead had slipped away leaving her face look so peaceful and her smile was gone forever.

"I'm too late," I said, feeling an anger beginning to grow in the pit of my stomach.

I roughly brushed away a tear and held on to her warm hand.

"Close your eyes," Aniya ordered.

"What?"

"Hurry, she's not got long." she ordered once more.

Confused, I closed my eyes and watched as the blackness dissolved to show a dark street leading to a bridge. It was quiet with no cars or people, except for the silhouette of a girl in a floor-length white dress. As I stepped closer, I realised she was stood at the edge where the side had been broken off. She was carefully looking down at the water.

"Annabella?" I whispered and as she turned to face me, I was winded by a mixture of relief and awe.

"Ayden..." she spoke softly.

I hurried over to her, taking each step quicker than the last and once I was within arms distance, I scooped the side of her face into my hand and pulled her lips to mine. As she began to kiss me back, every hair on my body stood tall. I quietly cursed myself for not seeing her sooner. I had wasted so much time telling myself I didn't have enough time, that I had lost it all anyway.

It was the feeling of her tears falling onto my face that brought me back to the ground.

"Is this real?" she whispered and I nodded.

"I think so, but we don't have long."

As the corners of her mouth formed into a smile, I felt my stomach tie itself into a knot.

"I'm sorry, Annabella, I shouldn't have ever..." I began to apologise, but was stopped as she placed an icy finger to my lips.

"Let's not waste the time we have left."

I nodded as she wiped a tear away from my cheek.

"I've never met anyone like you in all my years. You truly are a one of a kind, Ayden, and I couldn't possibly thank you enough for what you have given me this past year." I stopped her, pulling her into me and placing another kiss on her.

It was me that should have been thanking her. I wanted to thank her for giving me a chance even after the way I had treated Effy. I wanted to tell her how grateful I was to be trusted with her secret and even after the way I had treated her these past few weeks, she still forgave me. The truth was, I didn't deserve to know Annabella Hart, but by some miracle I did and it broke my heart a million times over that I had to let her go.

"I can't believe this is it." she said, taking herself out of my arms and facing the black water beneath us.

"Annabella, when we were in Madrid at that bar, you asked me to dance. I would really like it if we could."

With tears rolling down her face, she nodded and took my hand before resting her head on my chest. As we moved around slowly on the dark and empty street, I inhaled her scent wishing I could bottle it up and take it with me forever.

"I'll never forget you, Annabella," I whispered as the sound of a clock began to chime loudly behind us.

She pulled away, but kept her hand in mine, "I'm so scared."

I slid my fingers in between hers and held tight, "Don't be. I am here and we'll do this together." I smiled and tried to swallow past the lump in my throat.

"Okay." she replied and all I wanted to do was take away her sadness and be the one that had to jump.

"Ready?" she spoke softly, looking up at me.

I took one more look at her and prayed that there would never be a day where I didn't remember her perfect face, her beautiful smile and the moments I would only ever share with her. There would be a day that I would love again, but nothing would ever come close to how I felt about Annabella Hart.

I squeezed her hand, raising it to my lips to kiss one last time as I felt a warm tear fall down my cheek.

"Ready."

Epilogue

AYDEN

"Can I get beer, please?" I half waved at the bartender as he looked irritated by me for interrupting him chatting up a girl at the end of the bar.

I slid into a booth — the same one I had found Annabella in a year and a half ago. It was the day she told me the truth for the first time and, despite being curious, I dismissed her claims.

"Here." The bartender grunted as he placed the beer in front of me a little too roughly as it slightly spilled onto the wooden table. The bartender returned back to the bar and resumed his flirting as I pulled apart an abandoned newspaper to wipe up the liquid. As the paper grew damp quickly, distorting the words and images, I noticed the date. I already knew it, of course.

How could I not? Today was the 28th March.

Looking at the watch that Michael Garcia had gifted me on my 19th birthday, I watched as the seconds flickered by, bringing the anniversary of her death closer. In six minutes time, Annabella would have been gone for a year and in that year everything had seemed to have changed.

Mum had been to rehab three times, but it had seemed that the third try had been the lucky one as she had recently collected her pin for her sixth month of sobriety. She had even taken up a job as a cashier in the local Sainsburys and was looking into studying midwifery. For the first time, people were believing that perhaps she might have finally turned a leaf, but no one dared to say it out aloud.

Michael was still around and we had fallen into a weird but comforting role as 'Father and Son'. His divorce with Effy's mum had finalised and Michael was now alone most of the time, forcing himself into work. I'd be lying if I didn't say I was worried about him sometimes. Once Annabella had gone and we buried Effy's body, I knew he needed me. He needed someone to take care of. Someone to be a dad to. So I tried my best to fill the ever-growing hole in his life.

School had finally finished and gone were the likes of Brogan and co. as they left for university or college, but truth be told, I no longer had an interest in them anymore, not since Annabella. Instead, I had taken a job offered by Michael as a PE assistant in my old school, promising that at the end of the school year I would use the money Annabella had left me to go and travel, but it just didn't feel right.

A lot didn't feel right anymore.

People kept saying that with time, things would get easier and it kind of did in the way that putting a plaster on a wound that needed stitches did.

I looked up at the TV in the centre of the room, showing the replays of a dancing show that I knew my mum watched every Saturday. As I watched the clock in the corner of the screen change to 00.00, I took a long gulp of the cool beer and reached for my phone buzzing in my back pocket.

Michael: Hope you are alright.

I quickly replied back the same, knowing he would be feeling the same.

00.01am.

A year ago, at that time, Annabella was gone and after jumping into the water with her, I woke up beside Effy's limp body knowing things would never be the same again.

"Mind if I sit here?" I noticed a pair of black heeled ankle boots appear near the table as the voice spoke. Following the shape of her body in black skinny leather trousers and a deep purple top that slightly flared out at the waist, I found long blonde curls surrounding a pale face.

"Well...?" she spoke again and I felt mesmerised by her blue eyes that seemed almost transparent.

"Can I sit here?" she repeated.

I pulled my eyes away before looking around the room to find most areas packed with weekend drinkers.

"Sure."

Trying to avoid talking to her, I pretended to focus on the TV screen as the dancers moved around, shaking their hips in red sequins. I vaguely recognised one of the dancers from a boyband.

"I used to be a professional dancer, not anymore though." The girl spoke as she tucked a stray curl behind her ear, watching the screen.

"Yeah, so did a friend of mine." I replied politely, debating whether to offer her a drink. As beautiful as she was, I didn't want anything to do with her, but felt compelled to stay put and speak to her.

"What was her name?" She asked.

"Sofia Martinez."

She nodded and looked back at the TV.

"Why did you stop dancing?" I kept my gaze on her.

"It was just time to stop." she replied before looking back at me with a smile that felt familiar. "Do you want to dance?" she asked so calmly, as though asking if I wanted a drink.

I laughed, "Here? In this bar..?"

"Why not?" She stared at me in a way that left me questioning myself, "After all, you do still owe me a proper dance..."

I frowned, wondering what she was talking about as a smile grew on her lips. It was as I became lost in her eyes again that I slowly realised.

"It's not possible." I whispered.

She bit on her bottom lip as her eyes began to glisten, "I think it is."

"Annabella?" I asked before she nodded. "How? You were dead, you have been dead... for a year... today."

She shook her head slowly, "No... I wanted to come sooner, but I needed to be sure this was... real."

I shook my head as she slowly climbed out of the booth and reached out a hand in front of me.

"So, about that dance..." She laughed before placing her hand on my shoulder.

I stared into her eyes as I cupped her cheek, unable to wait any longer before I slowly leaned in. My other hand was slightly trembling as the sound of my heart pounded so loudly that I couldn't concentrate on anything but her face. As our lips finally touched, I could have sworn that sparks had begun to fly all around us as the world seemed to slowly begin to mend itself.

It wasn't the most passionate kiss we had shared, but it

was the most intimate as we moved in perfect sync as though no time had been lost.

"How many days do we have?" I said tearing myself away from her lips, recognizing the familiar dread in the pit of my stomach.

Annabella smiled as she wrapped her arm around my neck before whispering, "This time, we have forever."

the end.

about
SARAH RIAD

364 Days a Year is Sarah Riad's second YA novel after releasing The Sharp Knife of a Short Life late 2017. When she isn't working on her books, Sarah works in the city of London juggling her time as a Legal PA and studying part-time for a degree in Psychology.

Let's be friends—follow me on social media.

SARAH RIAD
young adult author

www.sarahriad.com

 facebook.com/SarahSRiad

instagram.com/SarahSRiad

ACKNOWLEDGEMENTS

How is it even possible I'm writing an acknowledgement for ANOTHER book?! After finishing and publishing my debut, The Sharp Knife of a Short Life, last year, I spent the following few months wondering whether I'd ever write again but then Annabella/Effy appeared and, as they say, the rest is history.

To anyone that thinks writing a book is a one-person job, you're wrong. In fact, you couldn't be more wrong. It takes the amount of people that are able to squeeze into a train on the central line during rush hour. Yes, I'm the one that actually writes it and it's all my idea but to make it into a pleasant reading experience with comma's in the right place and words that actually exist, you need an army.

So without further ado, a huge thank you to those below that made this book possible:

Megan - You are so important to this book and to me. This book wouldn't be here without you. I'm incredibly grateful for your friendship and I can't wait for our next chapter!

Samantha, Molly, Avneet, Alex, Yasmin and Kerry - Thank you for your ongoing support and pushing me to continue with this story. It goes without saying that your friendship means so much to me!

My editor, my proofreader, cover designer and formatter – Thank you for understanding what I wanted to achieve with this book and being patient with my many requests.

My ARC Team - I can't thank you all enough. I honestly write these books never expecting anyone to read them but you guys signed up without knowing a single thing about the book - some of you hadn't even seen the cover! Thank you for the kind words, the messages of support, the on-going encouragement and for giving this book a chance!

Bookstagram & the Online Book Community - A place where I've found new friends, new authors and pages I'd never have known about. Thank you to everyone that has ever messaged me, commented and shared a post - you're all such amazing people!

The IT Twosome – You know who you are and you both never fail to make me laugh! Thank you for everything and I told you that you'd be in the book - ha!

Last but not least, to anyone that reads this book, whether you bought it or borrowed it, whether I know you or not, there isn't enough ways to thank you - you make a nobody feel like a somebody.

Please enjoy the following excerpt from Sarah Riad's debut
novel...

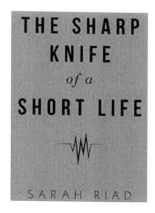

CHAPTER

one

DEATH.

Death found me at school, he sat beside me and told me his name. He soon shared my friends, some who would stare at him longingly, writing his name above their own surrounded by an uneven heart. And yet, despite all their best efforts, it was obvious Death only had eyes for me.

Noah, that's Death's name. He was the reticent transfer student that just appeared one day and would leave just as he arrived - no questions ever actually answered.

Life before Death was pretty unspectacular. I lived what I imagined to be the definition of a fairly average modern-day life. Mum, step-dad, twin brother, little sister and a missing dad. We lived in a beautiful family home in London which my mum took care of leaving the cleaner who visited every Sunday almost redundant.

I attended sixth form with my brother, Miles, where we sat on the opposite ends of the grading system. I studied English Literature and Latin Studies in hope of being accepted at Oxford University which would have put me on the path to teach or even better, become a writer.

You could say that I was part of the popular group at school, but no one on earth would have ever considered me as one of the cool kids. When people looked over at our table at lunch, or outside the gates after school, I would always be the one that raised eyebrows. I was the girl that would show up to the white party wearing all black.

In the modern day, to be considered popular in school you needed money to buy the latest Apple product or designer handbag, striking good looks that were Instagram worthy and the all-important contacts. The majority of my friends were all of the above. I, however, was none.

There was an exception to the rule though. You could become popular by impressing the group with some skill or talent that they could manipulate. Example? Bradley Johnson was not particularly good looking nor did he have access to unlimited money but he did make the best fake ID's. That made Bradley needed, and in return, he became popular. Well, it did until people reached 18 and then he would become useless, but then that was supply and demand.

That wasn't how I got included into the group either.

So, how does little old me with no model-like beauty, an Instagram account with 43 followers and no useful skills except for the ability to decipher the language of Shakespeare become part of the popular group? Well, this is where you meet Francesca Smyth. My best friend.

Frankie was always going to be popular. Where to start? She was stunning, and I mean the kind of beauty that make up spoiled. Frankie should have been a model; it was an injustice to the world that she wasn't according to her mother who had spent the past year trying to convince Frankie's father to let a prestigious modelling agency sign her up. He had adamantly declined, but that didn't stop Frankie from being the envy of everyone that knew her. If her full smile and large almond shaped eyes didn't impress you, then her parent's vast wealth and indirect connections to the Royal family would.

Frankie and I began sixth form in the same house and on our very first day we were paired up as each other's house buddy. Whether it had originally been sympathy or genuine fondness, Frankie forced me under her wing, and despite our lack of shared interests and very different upbringings, we would soon become inseparable.

Fast forward two years later, I had a full membership to the popular group without having ever applied or with any of the necessary skills.

I wasn't a complete bore though; I did join them for a few parties throughout the year, aiming for the bigger and more special occasions, like a birthday or their parent's Summer/Christmas parties.

It had taken all of Frankie's best efforts over the last two years to try and make me into a lesser version of her. She was always fascinated with making me see my 'full potential'.

"You really should try this mascara; it would make those gorgeous hazel eyes of yours stand out".

I had sat through many of makeovers where my long and wavy brown hair was transformed into a head full of loose curls, and my lips were smothered in red lipstick that would always end up on my teeth. I would argue myself out of the skin tight red mini dress with little care of the £2,000 price tag attached to it, and we'd finally agree on one of her less 'naked' dresses leaving a bit more to the imagination and not resulting in an evening of me trying to cover up my dignity.

My feet would be shoved in heels that carried a death sentence, and I would be spritzed with an entire bottle of perfume. Frankie would look at me with pride, clapping her hands in excitement and only occasionally frowning at my attempts to pull the dress down.

It wasn't just at school did wealth and beauty get you into the 'cool clubs'. The same rules applied to the renowned nightclubs in London. Alone, my attempts at getting into a club would end as soon as it started. Of course, being 17 would scupper my plans and warrant a smug shake of the head from the John Cena wannabe door-man. But with Frankie and co by my side, I was allowed to glide right through without so much as a glance. I wasn't too bothered though and was quite content that my visits to those particular places were few and far between.

Frankie and everyone else had begrudgingly accepted that I would always prefer my flat shoes to sky high Louboutin's and my Jane Austin novels to glossy Vogue magazines. I was the girl next door, dependable and consistent which was why we were all at a loss when Noah White came strolling into school and made me the subject of his attention.

Little fact, Noah prefers to be called Noah and not Death. "Do you go by the name of Darcey or shall I just call you 'student' or perhaps just 'person'?"

He also didn't like 'Angel of Death' and in no way was I ever allowed to call him the Grim Reaper. I am not entirely sure I see the difference in the titles as they all meant the same thing to me but hey, he is the expert.

Before all of this, I had rarely thought about dying, I mean, who does at 17 years old? On the rare occasion you might, it would be a fleeting moment when you had heard of a famous person dying or an old grandparent which hardly left you thinking, "Oh no, it's me next!"

The thing is, we rarely hear about child deaths. Yes, we hear about the babies that die prematurely due to complex health issues or congenital disabilities, but we never hear about adolescent deaths that happen every day. It's always that one kid that has the incredibly rare terminal illness that you hear and watch videos about on Facebook. Yes, it's a tragedy, but you'd be a fool if you thought they were the only one.

What if I told you that in 2015 alone, 1.2 million adolescents died in the world, would you still believe it was uncommon?

The majority of us spend our entire childhoods being told that only old people die and that we will most likely live forever. Parents try their hardest to hide a child away from death as though it were the boogeyman or something from a horror film. It's completely forgotten or perhaps ignored that death is more certain than life itself. It's natural and inevitable, and yet adults continue to hide us from it so that when we are forced to face it, we have no idea what to do.

I'm not saying you should run up to your children now and tell them their death could be imminent but you do at least owe them the PG version of the truth.

My grandad, Jasper, died two years ago at 85 years old. He wasn't sick or senile but just one evening decided that was his last. My nan, Hetty, was devastated but said it was time for his old soul to find its way to the angels. My mum said he would turn into a ghost and make his way up to heaven. An episode of Tom & Jerry told me that you'd have to walk up thousands of shiny gold steps before you reached a golden gate where your fate would be decided. Good and you would be let in, but if you were bad, you would fall back down the stairs into a fiery hell.

Of all the myths and stories I had been told, not many included Death, the Grim Reaper or the Angel of Death showing up. The idea of the Grim Reaper only came up when watching a horror film or on Halloween when someone would come out with the trusty black cloak and plastic scythe. You certainly wouldn't have picked Noah out of the list to play the part.

To you and me, Noah was just a regular person, an average 19 year old, no different to any other boy in school. He styled his dark brown hair messily to one side, and he looked through breath-taking emerald eyes but, it was his smile that stole the stares. The way his full lips would fall into a crooked grin with a dash of mischief.

"I used to work on my parent's farm with my brothers," He explained. "but I died about 75 years ago when I was 19."

I did the math's and was stunned to be looking at someone that could have been 94 years old. I pictured Noah still married to his sweetheart after many decades and playing with his grandchildren the way he did with April.

Noah rarely spoke about his past, but when he did, it was always as if it was by accident, almost forgetting who he was and most importantly, why he was there.

"Excuse me, here is your nose. I found it in my business." He would usually say, withdrawing as soon as he thought he had said too much.

Consider it a good day or a case of chance but one day, I asked him what Death's purpose was, and by some miracle, he began to answer.

"At the moment where life and death meets, we arrive and collect the soul."

I daren't ask a question in fear he would stop.

"But sometimes, we have to do a little more than just show up. You see, each person is different, and no two people deal with death in the same way. Maybe they have just had a car accident, and they are in a severe amount of pain. They are terrified of what is happening to them and what might happen next. That is when we arrive and take away the pain. We soothe the fear and stay with them so that they are never alone.

Or maybe, someone has received the news of their impending death and simply need someone to remind them of their courage to keep going on, even when they are at breaking point. When that moment comes and they need us most, we give them comfort and a reminder of their strength to carry on. We can be a presence or even a simple smell. The beauty about humans is that they don't always have to see someone to know they aren't alone."

I wondered if that was why some people claimed to sense the ghost of a loved one.

"Does that mean those that have passed away can come and visit us?" I asked, pushing my luck.

He ignored me, but he also didn't stop.

"Those that don't need us at all don't see us until the very end, in those last final moments. When they are taking their last few breaths and see nothing but blurred outlines and darkness, that is when we appear. Have you ever seen when a person is dying, they reach out to someone? That's us that they are reaching out to because they know why we are there. At that final point, life and death is merged, the person is no longer aware of their surroundings. They have no idea where they are, but they don't care because they can see us." "But what about those that call out the names of those that have passed, I have seen it in films, and my mum said my grandad kept calling his mother's name?"

He studied my face, and I could see he was trying to decide whether to answer.

"Not everyone is given this job but those that do have, or at least had, family at some point."

I smiled, wondering if one day I could be collecting my family members.

"Hang on, does that mean that my grandad wasn't given the role or wouldn't he have come to get me?"

He looked over at me frowning, "far too many questions, Dawson, far too many."

I had mirrored his expression before he gave in with a slightly twisted smile, "Well it is that, or he declined the offer, and I am starting to see why he might have..." I swung my arm back hitting his chest, and he feigned great pain before facing the TV again.

In the beginning, the questions never ceased. As I would ask one, twelve more would appear, all as important as each other and most receiving the same reply...

"there your nose goes again."

I could have killed him. Could he not appreciate the situation I was in, faced with Death himself but unable to ask a single question.

He told me several times that eventually everything I found so important would no longer mean a thing and, in time, I would find I had far more important questions than what heaven might look like.

He was right, of course.

Soon enough, the questions ceased altogether. It didn't matter anymore if hell existed and if there were such thing as angels. The questions didn't matter because I no longer cared for the answers. My story was always going to have the same ending.

I wish I could say that I knew I was dying from the moment I fell ill and that I had a gut feeling something was wrong. The truth is, I had no idea. In fact, I was so sure it would tip the other way, and I would be okay. I was young, fit and healthy, why wouldn't I fight it? The doctors were positive, and I was reacting well to treatment. Of course, the whole experience had made me conscious of death, but life was very much my focus.

It was Noah who told me, not that I was sick but that I was eventually going to die. I remember as he said the words, I lost the sense of my hearing first and then a tingling sensation in my fingertips begun to spread across my body. My heart raced, thumping furiously against my ribs and was soon greeted by the rise of bile. I had been back home on a short break for four days when he told me.

"Are you crazy? How can you say that to me? Who says that to someone who is sick?"

Bear in mind that, at the time, I had no idea Noah was anything more than just a regular kid who may or may not have fancied me.

I could see the regret on his face straight away as he wished he could have reversed time by a few minutes and take it all back.

"Get out now!" I screamed so loud that it burned my throat as the feeling of warm tears spread across my cheeks. I couldn't tell you why I was crying. If it was the shock, the anger or whether for a second I believed him. Why on earth would he say such a thing if it weren't true? This was Noah, the boy that had been with me from the very beginning of my illness, who sat in the hospital most days helping whenever he could. He had done everything to prove he had cared about me, so none of what he said had made sense. Why would he have wanted to hurt me?

"Darcey, I am sorry, I wish I didn't have to do this."

I looked at him in genuine shock, wondering if I had made friends with a crazy person.

"I'm sorry Darcey."

I shook my head in rage and pointed to the door, "get the hell away from me, get out of my house and don't you dare come back!" I could see my hand shaking in the air.

He pursed his lips together tight and slowly walked towards the door, stopping as he stood beside me.

"I wish I were wrong, I do Darcey, but I'll prove it to you. Tonight." His face was serious, and I could see he believed every word he had said.

"And how the hell are you going to prove I am dying tonight?!" I tried to mock, but all you could hear was fear.

I could hear him open the front door and before he closed it, he spoke loud enough for me to hear in the gentlest of voices, "Because I'm Death."

He broke two rules that day. First, telling me, I was dying and then, telling me he was Death. To this day, he has never told me why but I could probably guess.

In the end, the only plausible conclusion I had come to was that Noah was going to kill me that night. It would be me that finally had a good-looking boy's attention and he would turn out to be a murdering psychopath.

I nervously laughed but don't for a second doubt that I didn't beg my mum to sleep with me that night.

At the time Noah revealed I was dying, my doctors were so positive that I was moments away from being able to announce I was cancer free. All that was stopping me was one last round of chemotherapy and a bone marrow transplant that my brother would give me. I was so close to a future... to my future, until that night.

Blue lights once again, wailing through London and then I saw Noah, and I knew, I was dying.

Since being diagnosed, I had found it quite fascinating how everyone had a different take on what dying was like, and it always seemed like those that had never experienced or witnessed it had the most to say about it. Everyone thinks they understand and they know what might help. Doctors believe that they can relate because science says so. Friends and family believe that they can relate because their uncles, friends, brothers, wife died a few years ago.

The truth is, people are just selfish, whether you see it as a good thing or not. We are selfish beings that always think of ourselves first.

How would I feel if that was happening to me? How would I want things if it was me in those shoes?

Some people are sensible, realising that we are all different and handle things in a variety of ways. They make an effort to try and cater to the person that is sick. While others do as they would want things, taking no consideration as to what it is that is needed.

"If it were me, I would hate the fuss, all that attention reminding me every day."

Come on, do you honestly think that making some fuss will have me remembering all over again that I am sick?

Dying is like the ocean, sometimes the tide comes in gently with soft, delicate waves quietly working in the background. Other days, the waves violently crash into explosions, demanding to be noticed but regardless of how it chooses to do its job, the tide will always come in.

I wake up in the morning with a sigh of relief, and I go to bed praying I get to do it all over again the next day. Ignoring me or making a fuss does not, and will never change that.

"You need to be a little more compassionate. They are just trying to understand." That's what my mum said.

They didn't get it though, they weren't. They just told me how I was supposed to act and feel.

If someone chose to spend a day in bed crying or drinking so much alcohol that they failed to remember any of the night, then please don't tell them how they will go on to regret that they didn't spend the day in a more meaningful way. What if that was the way they wanted to spend it? What if their regret was that they never had the chance to get so drunk that they forgot their name?

I had a therapist to help me come to terms with my fate. Her name was Victoria or Dr Harrison and never Vic or Vicky. Straight away, you got the sense that Victoria was very professional. She dressed immaculately in creaseless grey pencil skirts and pretty white blouses. She also wore pointy heels which I always tended to associate with a serious business woman. It's not like you see a lawyer walking around in a pair of 6-inch platforms. Victoria had the posture of a ballerina and the strut of a Next Top Model, and yet her features couldn't have worked harder to change your opinion. She had these huge pale blue eyes that looked at you softly as though she only ever had kind thoughts and when she smiled, childlike dimples would appear.

Victoria was my third therapist, and with all, I had started the first session with asking them what their definition of 'acceptance' was. You see, I wanted to know that I was confiding in someone who was at least reading from the same page as me. My previous therapists had not even been in the same genre, let alone the same book.

"Well, it depends on what you are asking me to accept? Am I being asked to accept that magic cleaning fairies do not exist and I will have to clean my house once I get home or am I being asked to accept I am dying?"

I listened carefully.

"I believe it is a matter of a person's perspective.

CHAPTER 1

Consciously, we are both aware that we are both going to die eventually. However, you have been told it's sooner than expected but it doesn't change the fact that we are both still dying, just you know roughly when. Yet, it is entirely possible that I could have an accident this evening and be faced with imminent death. That is something we are all aware of, whether subconsciously or not."

"So, do you believe there are different levels of acceptance?"

She remained unmoved, keeping her gaze on me.

"What do you think, Darcey?"

"I think you can tolerate a difficult situation."

"But isn't tolerance simply another word for acceptance?" I stayed silent.

"Tell me, what is your definition of tolerance?" She crossed her long legs.

"I think it's the capacity to endure difficult circumstances while still wanting to change your fate".

Victoria nodded.

"Then answer me this Darcey, are you tolerant of your situation?"

I didn't reply, and she knew that I wouldn't. We both knew the answer already.

Was I tolerant of the fact I was sick?

Yes.

Was I tolerant of the fact that my fate was never going to change?

No.

Want to know more? Buy it on Amazon!

Printed in Great Britain
by Amazon